...e for...' He broke off and almost looked uncomfortable. 'Me.'

His lips thinned as he turned back to glare at her. She was used to full-on media 'glare,' but his dark-eyed look was just about the fiercest, most cutting scrutiny she'd had to withstand.

'I'm—'

'Sorry,' she snapped. 'The word you're looking for is *sorry*.'

'Tired,' he said firmly. 'I'm tired and I made a mistake. And I'm *sorry*, but you can't stay here.'

She needed this bed.

'Look.' She abandoned all dignity and pride. 'We can figure something out. I'll take the floor.'

Rigid, his glare pierced deeper. It was a wonder her bones didn't snap from the force emanating from him.

'You are *not* sleeping on the floor.'

Implacable? Yeah—he had the whole stubborn attitude on.

'Fine.' She switched tack. 'We'll share.'

Dear Reader,

There are very few people who aren't entranced by twins. My twin daughters delight and amaze me every day, and when they were babies I was frequently stopped by people wanting to take a closer look. I feel so privileged to have them, and it's fun to see how two people who can appear to be so alike are in reality so very different. That idea tied in nicely with another 'perception and reality' theme that intrigues me—how someone's public persona can be very different from the private truth.

So when it came to planning this new trilogy, I thought it would be fun to create identical twin heroes and, to add an extra twist, give them a brother less than a year older. Can you imagine the chaos three boys so close in age could create? And then when they're wickedly charming adults—who could resist?

James, George and Jack Wolfe are ambitious, arrogant, gorgeous. Raised to be risk takers, ultra-adventurous James is the one who endangers himself most—physically, at least. Going from disaster zone to disaster zone, he's a bona fide hero. But, courageous as he may appear, the one thing he isn't willing to risk is his heart.

I had so much fun putting the ultimate feisty threat in his way. Caitlin, a woman desperate to shake her bad-girl rep and escape her past, destroys James's quest for emotional isolation.

Their private tease—and moments of truce—were such fun to write, I hope you laugh as much with them as I did. And be sure to keep an eye out for George's and Jack's stories to come in early 2014!

With very best wishes,

Natalie

WHOSE BED IS
IT ANYWAY?

BY
NATALIE ANDERSON

First published in Great Britain 2013
by Mills & Boon, an imprint of Harlequin (UK) Limited,
Harlequin (UK) Limited, Eton House, 18-24 Paradise Road,
Richmond, Surrey TW9 1SR

© Natalie Anderson 2013

ISBN: 978 0 263 91056 8

Harlequin (UK) policy is to use papers that are natural, renewable and recyclable products and made from wood grown in sustainable forests. The logging and manufacturing processes conform to the legal environmental regulations of the country of origin.

Printed and bound in Spain
by Blackprint CPI, Barcelona

Natalie Anderson adores a happy ending, which is why she always reads the back of a book first. Just to be sure. So you can be sure you've got a happy ending in your hands right now—because she promises nothing less. Along with happy endings, she loves peppermint-filled dark chocolate, pineapple juice and extremely long showers. Not to mention spending hours teasing her imaginary friends with dating dilemmas. She tends to torment them before eventually relenting and offering—you guessed it—a happy ending. She lives in Christchurch, New Zealand, with her gorgeous husband and four fabulous children.

If, like her, you love a happy ending, be sure to come and say hi on Facebook, www.facebook.com/authornataliea, and on Twitter, @authornataliea, or her website/blog: www.natalie-anderson.com.

For Sylvie and Evelyn, two pieces
of pure delight in my life

CHAPTER ONE

NEW YORK, THE city that never slept. James Wolfe never slept either—at least not in planes, trains or automobiles. And with back-to-back long-haul flights, horrendous delays and now traffic at a time when in any other city there wouldn't be any, he'd gone more than forty hours without and was about to flip. Only a few more minutes and he could fall into bed. *His* bed—no hostel bunk, no hotel bed, no hastily built bivvy in a newly popped-up tent city. He couldn't wait. He willed the traffic to part to let the taxi keep on moving. To take him home.

'You been travelling?'

Given the cabbie had picked him up from the airport, this was obvious. But James automatically pulled on a smile. The guy had recognised him and James wasn't about to burst bubbles by being rude. Uncomfortable as it was, public attention was now part of the deal. So he nodded and tried to speak. But the words wouldn't come together in his strung-out mind.

'Can't talk about it, huh?'

James slowly shook his head.

'You look beat.' The cabbie didn't seem to expect a reply to that.

Finally the car pulled up outside his apartment building. The cabbie offered to help James with his bag. Given all he had was a small carry-all it really wasn't necessary. He managed the 'no thanks' with a smile. Then the guy wanted to give him the ride free of charge.

'If you know who I am, you know I'm good for it.' James pulled out a last burst of comprehensible speech along with the dollars from his wallet. 'But you're working the late shift. You probably need to get paid…' His family probably needed him to.

The cabbie reluctantly nodded. 'Any time you need to go anywhere…' He took the cash and handed James his card. 'Thanks, man. You're—'

James widened his smile and got out of the cab before he could hear it. He didn't want to be that good guy, that 'hero'. All he was, at this point in time, was tired.

He waved a hand at the security guy, then took the elevator up to his floor. The wave of exhaustion rose right along with the floor numbers. Bone-deep relief hit as he quietly went into the condo and dropped his bag just inside the door. He didn't bother switching the lights on, the dimness soothed his tired eyes. It took them only a moment to adjust, though there wasn't anything to see anyway. The place had been stripped bare, ready to be completely refitted. He walked through the empty lounge, toeing off his boots as he went and unbuckling his belt and stepping out of his trousers. There was only one place he was headed and he was going straight there. He slowly hauled up the internal stairs, hoping his instructions had been carried out. That on the top level he'd find his bedroom and en-suite bathroom fully refitted, furnished, finished. Ready for occupation.

Two seconds later he stood at the foot of the bed, rubbing his raw eyes. But they weren't deceiving him. The bed was made up all right. A big, brand-new bed with acres of soft-looking white coverings. He felt the thick pile of a luxurious rug under his bare feet. He was certain that if he looked, his bathroom would be gleaming and perfect. But there was something else looking gleaming and perfect: a woman. A beautiful woman was curled up asleep right in the middle of his huge bed.

She'd left the blinds open so the city lights gave the room a pale glow. It made her arm and face luminescent. Her long blonde hair was spread enticingly in a swathe over the pillow. A golden beauty in his bed. Goldilocks herself.

He was dreaming.

He glanced around. There was no bag. No clothes anywhere. The rest of the room was pristine. There was just that too pretty, random woman in his bed.

Definitely dreaming.

Real life wouldn't be so cruel to have her actually there. Not at a moment when he had no chance of stringing a sentence together. No chance of talking, let alone doing any of the other things suddenly running through his head.

Ah, hell. He was overtired and had gone without sex too long and now his mind had come up with the ultimate 'willing-woman-lying-waiting' fantasy.

He blinked a couple more times but the vision didn't dissipate. He cleared his throat. She remained still.

Testing, he spoke. His voice rough and low. 'Sweetheart, wake up.'

She didn't wake, but the faintest of furrows appeared between her eyebrows.

Huh, fantasy girl reacted.

So did his body. Hell, she was gorgeous. But this couldn't be. He ached to be unconscious.

'Time to leave, darling.' Oddly he found himself whispering, almost not wanting the mirage to shatter. Maybe she could stay asleep and he could crawl in beside her. He only needed a few hours' shut-eye, then he'd be up to talking...and taking.

But her eyes shot open. He saw her focus quickly, right on him. With a gasp she sat bolt upright, clutching the sheet to her chest. Her lips remained parted, as if she was going to scream. But no sound came out.

It was James who dragged in the audible breath. His attention arrowed to her full, shiny lips. In the dim light he imagined they were slicked with some kind of gloss. Flavoured? Maybe cherry or vanilla? He did like vanilla. Yeah, it had been way, way too long if he was off sidetracking like this.

'Who are you?' he asked, rougher than he meant to.

Big, slumberous blue eyes blinked back at him. Her blonde hair tumbled about her sweetheart-shaped face. She looked warm and flushed and *ready*. A beautifully pliant, silken, tempting woman.

'Who are you?' he repeated, almost plaintively. This so wasn't fair. If this was a dream, he should have more energy.

'What do you want?' she asked, her voice husky.

'Uh…' Dear heaven, this just *had* to be a dream. A full-scale, torturous sexy dream. She was willing to do whatever he wanted? Asking him in that sultry voice? 'Um… honey, I can't do this right now…'

She stared at him for a long moment. He noticed her shoulders eased as she spoke with a breathy sigh. 'You're James.'

She knew that? She whispered his name in that honey-eyed-tone?

Pure fantasy.

'Yeah and I'm sorry, darling,' he said gruffly. 'As gorgeous as you are…as good as I know you'd be…it's not going to happen tonight.' No matter how pretty she was, he was never going to manage it.

She blinked and didn't move. Just stared at him. Hard. The flush in her cheeks deepened.

A weird prickling sensation pinched at the base of James' spine.

Her frown returned—a whole lot bigger than before. 'George told me to come here.'

Huh? Why were thoughts of his brother encroaching on his fantasy?

'George sent you here for me?' he asked, confused. The prickling sensation turned icy. Was she here because she'd been told to, or because she'd been *paid* to?

No way. This whole thing wasn't even real. And George would never set something like that up. He might have been going on at James to 'get back in the game' for months, but he'd never think *paying* for a playmate was a solution. The idea was insane. But James' fuzzed-out brain couldn't figure anything any more. He just wanted to be in his bed. Now. He closed his eyes, reckoned she'd be gone when he opened them again.

She wasn't.

And *her* eyes had narrowed, her expression tightened, her pixie chin lifted. 'You think I'm waiting for you?' she asked.

Wasn't she? This was all just some wonderful, weird dream, wasn't it?

He opened his mouth. Shut it. Swallowed.

Shit.

Caitlin Moore tilted her head back and stared at James Wolfe. She didn't think she'd ever seen such dark brown eyes—almost black, bottomless. Eyes a woman could drown in. Way darker than his twin's—George had more golden lights in both eyes and hair. But the main difference between the two was more obvious than that.

The scar snaked out from James' hairline, slashing across his upper cheekbone. She knew how he'd got it. You'd be hard pressed to find a man, woman or child in the world with Internet access who hadn't seen that iconic picture of James Wolfe running through the middle of a landslide struck village, ignoring the blood pouring down his cheek from the gash at his temple as he carried that broken child to safety. He'd been the one to operate on the kid himself. The hero. The ultimate good guy who thought *what*, exactly, about her?

Deliberately she didn't stare at the scar. Nor did she lower her gaze to stare at the legs he had on show. Or the bronzed arms appearing out of the grey tee that fitted him so much better than the one she wore. But she was aware of his tan, his obvious strength, his size. He was all weary warrior with those muscles, that stubble and the end-of-the-fuse glint in his eye. Well, she had her own fuse burning—*as good as he knew she'd be?*

'Who are you and what did George tell you?' he asked. He looked both confused and...*intense.*

James Wolfe was a medic, a rescue man. A hero who worked in disaster-ravaged countries. She knew exactly who he was. She knew all those amazing things about him. But he had no idea who *she* was, where she'd come from. Nothing about the recent nightmare she'd left in London. He'd not read the headlines, the worst of the bile from the Internet. So wasn't it just typical that even someone so 'good' automatically doubted her? Did he honestly think she was his paid plaything for the night? That she was here for his personal use and pleasure?

Caitlin sucked in a breath. Unhelpfully the air burned her lungs. She was already hot enough—with anger, right?

'You think I'm here to do whatever you want me to?' Caitlin ditched the sheet to reach out and flick on the reading lamp. She remained on the bed. Possession was nine tenths of the law and this was *her* sleep space tonight.

He didn't answer. Instead he stood frozen at the foot of the bed, staring at her with those wide, bottomless, ninety-eight-per-cent cocoa eyes. Finally a half-strangled sentence emerged. 'You're wearing my T-shirt.'

What, and that then made *her* his property?

With the light on, Caitlin saw the flush deepening in his upper cheeks and the tension humming through his body—pulling him taller, tighter. Bigger. Her eyes widened as she saw the interest in his. To her horror she felt recip-rocal heat build inside. She breathed out, hoping to cool it. No way. No *way*.

But was the guy attracted to her?

No. She mentally clarified. Not *her*. It was what he could see. What was with the Paleo instinct that kicked in when men saw skin? Insta-lust central.

Mind you, at this moment she might be found guilty of the same crime. All the muscles and skin he was showing were sure having an effect on her basic instincts. Not that he needed to know it. Not when he'd made such an out-of-line assumption.

'Be grateful I didn't take a pair of your boxers,' she said coolly. 'It was a close-run thing.'

'My...?' He stopped and swallowed. 'So what else *are* you wearing?'

He almost looked pained. And Caitlin couldn't resist the urge to turn the screw a little tighter.

'Just your T-shirt.' She faked a careless shrug and glanced towards the bathroom. 'My clothes are drying.'

His slightly glazed focus didn't leave her body. '*Just* my T-shirt?'

'I figured you had more than enough to spare.' There were about twenty in that walk-in wardrobe. All neatly pressed and stacked and exactly the same colour.

He blinked, clearly unable to get his head together. What

was the guy—all animal? Yet she was certain he wasn't. Oddly, despite her near nudity, despite the bizarreness of the situation, she didn't think for a second that she was in any real danger. So she wasn't afraid to bite.

'Who'd have thought that James—hero with a capital H—Wolfe likes to have a woman of ill repute waiting for him in bed when he gets back from his oh-so-honourable missions?' she said. It was unbelievable.

He stared at her with that dazed-and-glazed look, obviously trying to process her words. Was he drunk or something?

'So, you're not here for...' He broke off and almost looked uncomfortable. 'Me.'

'No, your brother did not pay me to come and be a sexual plaything for you.' Caitlin smiled sweetly. 'And don't you think—' she cocked her head '—that if I were such a "professional", I'd have chosen to be in your bed wearing something a little more sexy than one of your thousands of identical T-shirts?'

Though the shirt was damn sexy on him—the grey bringing out the depth in his eyes and the fit stretching across his chest in a seriously pulse-pounding fashion.

His lips thinned as he turned back to glare at her. She was used to full on media 'glare', but his dark-eyed look was just about the fiercest, most cutting, scrutiny she'd had to withstand.

'I'm—'

'Sorry,' she snapped. 'The word you're looking for is sorry.'

'Tired,' he said firmly. 'I'm tired and I made a mistake. And I'm *sorry* but you can't stay here.'

Okay, maybe she was a little in the wrong here too, given the guy actually owned a third of this apartment. But she couldn't afford to go anywhere else. And with her only clothes hanging wet in the bathroom? *Damn*.

Because worst of all she needed this space for more than piffling money reasons. She needed to hide. 'Well, it's just that your brother said I could stay for the next month.'

'Month?' His jaw fell open. 'No. No. No.'

Yeah, she already got that her month wasn't going to happen. But she needed to buy time to find a new plan. 'Well, I'm not going anywhere else tonight.'

'You have to.'

She needed this bed. George had said she could use it. But Grumpy James here was going to ruin it for her.

'Look.' She abandoned all dignity and pride. 'We can figure something out. I'll take the floor.'

Rigid, his glare pierced deeper. It was a wonder her bones didn't snap from the force emanating from him.

'You are *not* sleeping on the floor.'

Caitlin sighed. 'Don't pretend to be all chivalrous now. I've seen the real you unmasked, remember? You know, the guy unsurprised to find what he thinks is a hooker in his home.'

'You are not sleeping on the floor.'

Implacable? Yeah—he had the whole stubborn attitude on.

'Fine.' She switched tack. 'We'll *share*.' She glanced at the massive mattress. 'The bed is big.'

'Not big enough.' He looked shell-shocked.

She swallowed. He was probably right. He was not short and he had shoulders broad enough for a nation's sorrows. But she had nowhere else to go. 'Plenty big enough,' she argued stoically. 'I'll have this small edge here. We'll put some pillows down and you can have the rest. Will that do?'

'No.'

'What, you have some Victorian sense of propriety now?' she said.

'I never pay for sex. Nor do I sleep with unwilling women.'

Caitlin stared at him, momentarily lost for words. What did he expect her to say to that? A horrendous sizzle slid over her skin as her body whispered the word she surely should deny—*willing. So willing.*

Oh, no, that just wasn't right. The guy might be gorgeous, but he was a jerk. He'd just thought she was a prostitute. She shook her head.

Mindless with exhaustion, James just wanted the talking to stop. The drama to stop. Damn it, he needed *everything* to stop so he could sleep. For a good twenty hours. He'd been going on less than three hours for the last three weeks and that was before the forty-hour travel hell. He was past it.

'Look, I can control my debauched urges enough not to attack you,' he slurred more than spoke.

This sure wasn't some 'paid-to-please' woman—she was doing everything possible to *displease* him. And he supposed he couldn't really blame her for that.

He felt bad. His whole body ached, especially his brain. But worst of all was the flicker of desire. He didn't want her to stay in his bed. Not her with her stunning legs and curves and sparkling-for-all-the-wrong-reasons eyes. It was impossible.

Because he *wanted* but shouldn't. Besides that, couldn't. And she most definitely *wouldn't*.

There was no making this bad situation better, not while he was this sleep deprived and frankly addled. He closed his eyes but she was still talking. Something about pillows and space again. Infuriating, sexy-as-hell creature.

'I'm tired,' he interrupted, holding his hands up as he surrendered. 'I'm sleeping. Talk tomorrow.'

He pitched face first onto the bed, gave over to the dark.

Caitlin stared at the man now sprawled out on his stomach. Sound asleep already, his limbs stretched out over a good three quarters of the bed.

She should have known it was too good to be true. Walking into this apartment only a few hours ago she'd been so excited. Sure, the rest of the place was unlivable, stripped back to bare, but then she'd climbed the stairs—and hit heaven. Up in the clouds, this beautiful, glass-walled white room offered the most incredible view of Manhattan. She'd stood at the window and looked out at the inspiring constructions of concrete, iron and glass, interspersed with the greenery of parks and the blue patches of sky. She'd felt free. Positive. Safe.

And now? Grumpy bear had returned to his lair.

She glared at him. He was too handsome for his own good with his dark hair, stubble, and long eyelashes. The thin scar marked but didn't disfigure—it told of courage, sacrifice, determination. His long legs and arms were obviously strong but not bench-press-addict bulky. Hastily she drew the sheet up to cover him. She didn't need to ogle the jerk. What kind of man automatically assumed a woman sleeping in his bed was there waiting only for his pleasure? An arrogant one who'd had way too many women, way too easily.

She drew in a deep steadying breath. Tried to consider her options. Drew a blank. Just what *was* she supposed to do now? She was so tired from the last few weeks' media nightmare, from the hellish flight over from London, from the hour-long battle with the airline over her lost luggage, from facing all these battles alone…

So *damn* tired.

She looked at the strong man lying so contentedly asleep

in the big bed. If she couldn't beat him, maybe she should just join him?

Caitlin jammed a couple of pillows right up next to him, refusing to note once more just how fine his body was. Then she slipped between the sheets on the small space on the other side and turned her back to him, curling herself into a small ball.

Just for tonight.

CHAPTER TWO

JAMES WOLFE SANK deeper into the decadent, erotic dream. He tasted sweet mixed with salt, felt heat and hardness contrast with softness and smiles. Saw aquamarine eyes shimmering with defiance and desire. Heard words whispered with a wild edge. He reached out, wanting to touch...

But his hand slid over a cold sheet.

He slowly opened his eyes, trying to drag his reluctant, relaxed mind back to the realm of reality. First thing he saw was the empty stretch of mattress beside him. Frowning, he blinked—certain his dream woman had been in bed with him.

Then he heard the sound of running water emanating from behind the closed bathroom door. He smiled. It was okay. She was in the shower.

But then his mind, so briefly and blissfully rested, froze. He stiffened, then sat bolt-upright as actual memory returned and shredded the remnants of fantasy.

There *had* been a woman in bed with him. A woman who'd worn his shirt and nothing else. A woman he'd thought was...*hell.*

His stomach curdled.

George had said she could stay here. George never invited random women to stay. Not for more than a night and not without him. Which meant this woman was special.

James rubbed his aching temples with tense knuckles as the blindingly obvious hit him.

She had to be his brother's girlfriend.

George had been single a while, earning a reputation as a slayer—'making up for lost time now he was off the leash' as all the blogger types sniped. James knew some of George's supposed escapades were fabrication, but not all. Still, it wasn't impossible to believe George might've fallen for a blonde with soft-looking lips, and blue eyes that widened in surprise and sparkled in annoyance. Uh-huh. *Why* George wanted her was easy to see. She was easy to want. But letting her stay in their private condo was more than want. That meant serious.

And what had James done? All but called her a whore and told her to leave. He winced. All class, he was. George was, rightly, going to be pissed. James was going to have to grovel. To both of them.

The sound of running water ceased and James tensed. Maybe he could convince her to forgive and forget the whole incident? But *how* to convince her? Throw himself on her mercy? Explain he was so exhausted he hadn't been thinking straight? Blame the stress of his last assignment?

He glanced down, frowning at the white cotton sheet covering him. He didn't remember sliding under it last night, which meant *she* must have—

An entirely inappropriate image flashed in his head. An entirely enjoyable one. Hell, he wished he'd never seen her legs, or how curvy her unfettered breasts looked in one of his T-shirts.

His clothes. *His* bed. *His.*

If she was Goldilocks, he was definitely the bear. But he hadn't done a very good job of chasing her away. She'd been way more defiant than that thief from the fairy tale. She'd been almost desperate to stay. He wondered why that was.

The door to the bathroom opened. She walked out, her expression guarded. James' innards shrivelled in excruciation. She couldn't look *less* like a hooker. Her pale face peeked out above the turtle-neck roll of a giant black sweater. Baggy black jeans hung on her, hiding the figure he knew was lithe. She'd scraped her wet hair into a function-over-form ponytail, the bedraggled twist nothing like the swathe of colour that had blanketed his pillow so enticingly. Given her pallor he guessed she'd not brushed any make-up on. Cloaked with an air of wariness, she looked smaller, tired. But still determined. Still sexy.

Yeah, part of him wanted to haul her back to his bed, strip her out of the oversized gear and help her relax enough to sleep soundly. She looked as if she needed it as much as he and he still had seven hours' straight sleep in him. He could forget the world with her. Make her forget her own name. And George's?

Guilt skewered his chest. What was he thinking? To contemplate—even for a second—messing with the woman his brother had sent here? Maybe he *was* screwed up after his last assignment. Maybe he'd seen too many hearts broken. Maybe he'd got so desensitised he'd forgotten what was right and what was wrong. Because this was wrong.

He shifted, tugging up the sheet for something to do, cursing himself for not getting up and dressing while she was in the shower. Glancing back up, he caught a flash in her gaze.

James saw emotional extremes all the time—inconsolable grief, terror, pity, relief. Apocalyptic events pushed people beyond human endurance. He knew the keening wails of distraught villagers who'd lost loved ones, homes, land—people who'd lost everything but the ability to breathe. He emotionally distanced himself from them. Had to. Couldn't get his job done if he felt every hurt along with them. But he wasn't used to someone looking at him as if she wanted him to disappear. Or as if she wanted to be the one to *make* him disappear. Usually people fell over themselves in relief when they saw him. So this was novel. And frankly?

Interesting.

Inappropriate again. He gritted his teeth. He needed to get his head together. Find out the facts. And get her to leave.

'I'm thinking we need proper introductions,' he said carefully. 'As you know, I'm James, but I didn't get your name last night—'

'Caitlin.'

Her voice was every bit as cool as her expression. Both set him on the boil. Caitlin *who*? Caitlin *why*? The temptation to tease was impossible to resist. 'You like wearing other people's clothes, Caitlin?'

The ones she had on now sure weren't hers. Three sizes too big and not nearly stylish enough for her figure.

Colour touched her cheeks. 'My luggage got lost somewhere between London and New York.'

Luggage? So she'd only recently arrived? 'So that's why you were wearing my shirt?'

She inclined her head. 'I'd washed my clothes and they were still wet.'

'Those are really yours?' His brows lifted. He caught the resurgence of defiance in her eyes and checked himself. Tempting as it was to bait, he wasn't supposed to be making this worse. 'Why didn't you tell me?'

'You weren't interested in listening.'

'You were too busy talking.'

'You were too busy assuming.'

'You were too—' He broke off. *Too tempting*—with her beautiful hair and long, lush legs. Of course he'd thought

NATALIE ANDERSON 23

of sex. Hell, what man wouldn't when he was beyond tired, who'd lived in hell the last three weeks on top of a previous assignment that had been shorter, but even worse. Confronted with that vision—a sleeping, soft, hot woman? The idea of losing himself in her vitality, in feeling *alive* for a moment before diving into a deep, ideally dreamless sleep?

Oh, hell. He was a sick unit.

'So you're heading out to get some new clothes?' He dropped the previous topic and aimed for something less inflammatory. Fingers crossed she'd find a new place to stay while she was out.

She looked away, studying the room. 'I'm hoping my bag will arrive today.'

'There are a ton of shops to tide you over,' he said, wondering the best way to bring up the topic of her and George.

'That's not why I'm here.'

Surprised, he frowned. She was in no hurry to go buy a new wardrobe? What woman didn't like to go shopping? He glanced at her worn outfit again and mentally kicked himself. *A woman who couldn't afford to.*

Was that why she'd resisted leaving last night? She couldn't afford to go anywhere else? The defiant pride beaming from her eyes showed she wasn't about to admit it. Fair enough.

'Why are you here?' he asked.

'Just for a holiday.'

'For a month?'

She nodded but he got the impression she was keeping something back from him. George had said she could holiday here for a month? To be fair, James really hadn't kept his family up to date with his itinerary. He figured this mess-up served him right. If she couldn't afford to go anywhere else, he was going to have to do the gentlemanly thing—especially given his brother had offered the place to her. Except James didn't want to stay somewhere else. This was as 'home' as it got for him. It offered him isolation. Peace and quiet—something he only ever needed for a couple of days in between assignments.

If she was here on the tourist ticket she'd be out sightseeing all day, dining out, dancing half the night in the clubs. They'd hardly notice each other, right?

Aside from the minor detail that they'd have to *share*. Only this one room in the apartment was in action and, while sharing a room would be bad enough, sharing a *bed* with his brother's woman was on the 'forbidden' list. Assuming she *was* his brother's woman?

'George said you could stay.' He drew his knees up and leaned forward to watch her reaction.

She nodded again, glancing away. 'But it's clearly inconvenient.'

He thought rapidly. If he chased off his brother's girlfriend, he'd never hear the end of it. As it was he got too much grief for not being involved with the family enough. To be the 'beast' who'd scared beauty out of the castle would be too much for his brothers to stand. Doubtless they'd stage an intervention. 'George doesn't open up to many people.'

'He's been a good friend to me.'

Friend. Was that all he was? James ran his hand through his hair and down to rub the back of his neck. If he'd bothered to be in touch with his brothers more, he'd know. He wouldn't have to ask. As it was, he did. 'You know him well?'

'Not intimately. Which is what you're really asking, right?' She shot him a look. 'What does it matter to you?'

His blood heated at her defiant spark. 'You really need me to explain?'

The inappropriate reply was out before he could think to stop it. And really, the fierce surge of desire needed no explanation. With those blue eyes, blonde hair, the legs, and the curves that called out to be admired. Held. Tasted. And as for the spirited tilt of her chin and the colour seeping into her cheeks…

'In some ways you're very like your brother,' she said, her voice rougher than before.

'But I'm not him.'

George, though he was trying hard to deny it, was a commitment man. A keeper for the right woman. James was definitely not. No matter how right the woman, *he* was all wrong. And knowing that, he probably shouldn't be thinking all things sexy about his unexpected house-guest. He probably should back off and be good.

Except he was tired of being good.

She angled her head, studying him. 'Does it bother you? People confusing you?'

They weren't identical but were so alike most people thought they were. Until recent times, when James' injury made it obvious. But the scar was superficial. Their real differences had been etched inside years ago when, because of James, a man had died and a family had been destroyed. That old cold feeling sluiced down his spine. He stiffened, pushing it out. He was over that. He was busy, content. Doing something with his life. Slowly he shook his head. 'Used to. But we're very different. Sometimes I wish I were more like him.'

'In what way?'

Caitlin watched a remote look cross James' face, then his smile twisted and a surprisingly wicked gleam sparked in his eyes. She couldn't help thinking he'd summoned the charm to scare away the devils.

She knew George Wolfe was the ultimate playboy. Charming, witty, a master at making women willing, biddable, all too easily beddable. Not that she'd succumbed.

And truthfully, she'd not received his interest that way, he'd felt pity for her rather than attraction. Because they had that one thing in common. They'd both felt the bite of the press, the judgment of the ill-informed masses.

Notoriety.

But all George had offered her was a safe haven—a hideaway. Turned out the cave came with the big, growly bear who wanted isolation to hibernate. And James Wolfe was more predator than playboy. For all his supposed heroism he had a streak of the hunter. She felt far more at risk here and now than she ever had with George—far more at risk of succumbing. Because James Wolfe, with his sleep-mussed hair, stubble and smoky eyes, was compelling.

'If I were more like George, I'd have no trouble telling you how well you wear my T-shirt.' His smile deepened, a small dimple appearing in one cheek. 'And how much I'm kicking myself for being so abrupt last night.'

Abrupt? He'd been more than abrupt.

'I hope you can forgive me,' he said, as smooth as molten chocolate.

She didn't trust anyone who said anything nice to her—certainly not a man. Not any more. She was sure that in the depths of James' equally molten chocolate eyes, she'd find calculation. 'Is that what you really want?' she asked bluntly.

'What I really want…?' he echoed softly.

Oh, she was not falling for his sudden smoothness. She knew what he was up to. 'You're worried I'm going to tell the world what a jerk *the* James Wolfe actually is?'

His concern was laughable. He clearly wasn't aware there was no way the world would ever believe *her*.

His chin lifted, his smile turned self-mocking. 'Not worried about the world, but I am a little concerned about what George might say.'

George would probably laugh.

'So,' she challenged. 'You thought you'd turn on the Wolfe charm and befuddle me so much I'd forget all about it?'

His brows arched high. 'I thought it was worth a try.'

He was so obviously joking—trying to tease them out of this embarrassing situation. But to have another guy faking flirt with her for his own gain? She couldn't raise a smile. 'Why?' she asked tartly. 'You need the world to think nothing but the best of you? Your ego is so huge you need every woman to want you?'

He paused, a small laugh escaping beneath his breath. 'No, I just wanted you to forget how rude I was. But if you want to want me, I guess that's okay too.' He shrugged.

'I *don't* want you.'

'No?' He adopted a farcically crestfallen look.

Suddenly she couldn't *not* laugh. 'You're appalling.' Last night she'd never have imagined he'd be so ridiculous. 'What would you have done if I said I did want you?'

'You calling my bluff?' His smile burst back.

'So it *was* a bluff.' She'd been right, the guy was only out to cover his butt. That hot appreciative look he'd sent her way before was an act. The 'explanation' of why her relationship with George mattered was his fear for his reputation. Not because he was attracted to her and didn't want to tread on his brother's toes. And she was *not* remotely disappointed by that fact.

His expression went bland enough to mask all manner of nefarious intentions—but his dark eyes danced. 'I can neither confirm or deny.'

'Well, I can't *conform*.' She shook her head. 'I won't be one of your millions of adorers.' She didn't care how many lives he'd saved, she wasn't worshipping him.

His chin lifted in a sudden movement, as if he were a

predator who'd just caught a whiff of tasty prey nearby. 'True,' he said thoughtfully. 'You're not like most women I meet.'

'I'll take that as a compliment, given you only seem to meet people who think you're the best thing ever. It strikes me you've gotten away with too much for too long.'

'I have?' he queried, his lips almost quirking into another of those smiles. 'So what are you going to do about it?'

Caitlin paused, counting to ten to douse the flicker of attraction. She was super glad her 'hideaway' flight clothes swamped her and hid the unreasonable reaction of her body to his. She was all tight, all hot. Perhaps she'd picked up flu on the flight?

She didn't want this trip to start fraught with failure. Yet it was already. Lost luggage. Random midnight roommate. Looming homelessness. Could it get any worse?

Actually, yes. She'd run away from worse. She could handle this. She might be screwed but she wasn't going to beg. She'd figure something out. She had in the past, she would now. She straightened her shoulders and sucked it up. 'I'll go to a hotel.'

'No,' he shot back surprisingly quickly. 'Hotels are awful,' he added. 'Soulless places. Stay here.' His eyes twinkled.

'There really isn't room.'

'Sure there is,' he said easily. 'We managed just fine last night, didn't we?'

Last night she'd lain there for ages, barely breathing before accepting the guy was making like a gigantic piece of Lego. Immovable, inanimate, so faultless he had to be plastic. She'd wished he'd snored or something—she'd wanted to find a flaw, aside from the fact he'd briefly leapt to an unflattering assumption. But even now, with the air of weariness he wore, with the shadows under his eyes and the stubble on his jaw, even with that raw scar, he was the most startlingly sexy man she'd met. So truthfully, she hadn't managed that well at all. But given how broke she was, she was going to have to cope. The question was whether he wanted to—and if so, why he would?

'You don't mind the state it's in?' She paused to clear the frog from her throat. 'Or being so squashed?'

'This is nothing.' He looked amused.

Of course, he'd have seen places in far worse messes and no doubt lived in greatly uncomfortable situations for months at a time. Because on that level, he was that hero.

'I have a twin. I'm used to sharing,' he explained. 'We used to have a line of masking tape down on the floor marking out the boundary. Pain of death if you crossed it.'

Caitlin could easily imagine the scene. But she knew he came from wealth. His family had created the world's most popular independent travel guides. A total dynasty, they sold millions of books each year. Surely he'd grown up in a huge house? Her innards softened; the guy was trying to make her feel better. But she wasn't going to let him get away with gross exaggeration. 'You didn't have your own room?'

'Course not,' he answered instantly. 'We fought, but we're brothers. Half the time Jack would be in there as well.' He chuckled. 'When we got older, sure, we had our own rooms. But we were really close.'

Were. She paused, wondering about why that was. But she wasn't going to pry about anything so personal. Besides, he was only sharing this to make her feel as if she weren't putting him out. 'And how long is it since the two of you shared a room?' she asked bluntly.

He laughed. 'About twenty years,' he conceded.

Hmm. 'So this arrangement...would be...brotherly?'

'Sure.' His eyes crinkled even more at the corners. 'I

really am used to sharing. Sometimes it's really cramped quarters when I'm on an assignment.'

'All the more reason for you to have your space now you're at home.' She really shouldn't stay.

'You don't take up that much space.' He grinned amiably. 'I like to curl up like a cat.'

Ha. 'I slept beside you last night. I know how much you stretch out.'

A rueful expression crossed his face. 'Did I leave you any room?'

'Less than an inch.'

'Sorry about that. We can do something better with the pillows.'

Caitlin pressed her lips together for a moment to suppress the heat suddenly flaring inside. She could well imagine his physical demands would be great. He was the kind to want more. To take more.

'I can't let you do this.' Ugh, her voice had gone husky. She cleared her throat. 'I'll disturb you.'

He hesitated for a moment. 'I can sleep through anything.'

Actually, she figured that was true. He'd been out cold last night. 'So you're suggesting that we—two total strangers—share this one room?'

'I am.' He shrugged his shoulders. 'It'll only be for a couple days at most. I'll be heading out on another assignment soon. You'll have the place to yourself the rest of your month.'

Given she had no back-up plan, what choice did she have? But there was that one thing and she couldn't *not* spell it out. 'You honestly think it can work given what you thought on seeing me here last night?'

'I was really tired. Not thinking clearly.' For the first

time he glanced away from her first. 'You can't blame me. I think most men look at you and think "sex".'

'Is that supposed to be a compliment?' she drawled acidly.

'Hey, I'm just a man.'

'But you're not, are you? You're not just any man.'

He looked back at her. 'I think you'll find I'm very much just a man.'

'Given that, I'm really not sure it's a good idea I stay here.'

He studied her silently. Then smiled gently. 'Sweetheart, you have nothing to worry about.'

Somehow—ridiculous as it was, given he was trying to reassure her—she felt even more insulted than she had last night. 'Sweetheart?'

He grinned. 'Sugar, honeypot…'

'You've obviously forgotten my name is Caitlin.'

'I haven't forgotten anything about you.' A glitter intensified the laughter in his eyes.

That kind of focus was enough to make any woman blush. She drew breath, fighting the flare of heat in her cheeks. 'Okay, I definitely can't stay here.' She'd be safer on the streets.

'Sure you can.'

'Not if you're going to flirt like a bulldozer,' she grumbled. She didn't want any man-attraction stuff in her life right now. She wanted *peace*.

He laughed. A deliciously low, warm, infectious sound. 'You don't like flirting?'

Caitlin fought to keep hold of her grump and not succumb to his charm. 'It's not appropriate.' He didn't even *mean* it.

He looked even more amused. 'You honestly don't think

a guy and a girl can share a room without…' He raised his brows.

Oh, now he was making her seem like some kind of sex-crazed spinster. 'It's not that but—'

'Ah, you *do* think I'm attractive.' He nodded in a confiding way, his grin absurdly boyish.

Confound the man, he was confusing her. 'You *know* you're attractive,' she answered almost crossly.

'I do?' He turned his head and ran a finger down the thick red welt of the scar that came out of his hairline, cut across his temple and sloped crookedly down his cheekbone. 'This is attractive?'

Caitlin stared first at the scar, then into his suddenly impenetrably dark eyes. Was there an edge of bitterness? He was insecure about it? When the world knew how he'd got it? What he'd gone through?

'Your eyes are attractive,' she said quietly. His eyes were lethal. And they were just the beginning.

He shook his head, his smile returning but a little twisted. 'My bank balance is attractive. So is my surname—the family connection. The fame.'

Fame didn't make him attractive to her. She knew fame cost—not with the clichéd sweat, but soul. Fame-craving people sacrificed their humanity. But she got the feeling he was as unenthusiastic about fame as she was.

'Are you trying to play the pity card?' She adopted a sassy tone to lighten the prickly moment. 'You're worried the only reason women want you is because of your assets, not your personality?'

'You tell me.' His lips twitched.

'I'm not stroking your ego.'

He chuckled warmly again. 'So you're *not* attracted to me.' He nodded again as he spoke. 'Guess that means we'll have no trouble sharing the room.'

Hmm. She considered his tactics and had to acknowledge he was good. She could be too, right? And she really couldn't afford to go anyplace else. 'And obviously you're not attracted to me,' she said with a small faux sniff.

He looked at her silently, the single dimple appearing again.

'Given you fell asleep before you even hit the mattress,' she added, vaguely piqued. 'And you were desperately saying *no*.'

His shoulder lifted, a scant apologetic gesture. 'I didn't want to have to be nice.'

Another wave of heat caught Caitlin by surprise. 'You didn't want to have to be nice—in bed?' She cocked her head, the provocative words tumbling from her tongue. 'If I were a hooker, wouldn't it have been *my* job to be nice? It would only have been about getting off for you. You could have done your thing in twenty seconds and we'd both have been happy.'

'That's not the way I have sex.' He drawled the words, but his eyes kindled to a quick scorching heat.

'Ten seconds would've been okay as well.' She tried to shrug. 'You don't need to feel bad if that's all you can manage.'

He leaned forward, his smile appreciative. 'I don't feel bad because I'm *always* nice to my partner.'

'But you get tired of having to be nice? Why?' She let herself look directly into his intense, intoxicating, eyes. 'You want to get naughty sometimes?'

The fire in his expression flared into an inferno. He flung back the sheet and stood up from the bed. 'I'm not allowed to get naughty,' he said softly.

Why ever not? 'But you'd like to?' she pointedly asked, refusing to glance down and check out his legs. Or recognise the rapid pounding of her pulse. 'Aren't you all man?

In control of your own destiny? If you want to be wicked, be wicked?'

'Things are never that simple.' He walked towards her.

'No?' She lifted her chin free of the rollneck of wool and fought the instinct to step back. 'Seems they are to me. See, I'm bad. Bad news for anyone who comes near.'

'You're bad news?' His eyebrow quirked, as if he didn't believe her.

'Oh, yeah.' In the last few weeks the gossip columns had been filled with it. Only because they needed some kind of cannon fodder to fill the inches of newsprint and populate their webpages with salacious scandal. They all needed a villain. This month, she was it. She'd forgotten how awful it was to be vilified. She'd thought she'd escaped it years ago. 'You're right not to be attracted to me. I'm the wild child who'll ruin a man.'

'I never said I wasn't attracted to you,' he replied calmly. 'And your supposed badness can't ruin me.' He whisked the grey T-shirt off and tossed it onto the bed. 'I'm bulletproof, didn't you know?'

She stifled a gasp at his gesture. At the expanse of skin he'd exposed. Yep, the bullets would bounce off those bristling muscles. Dear heaven, this man was hewn.

'Nothing you can do could tarnish my image,' he said boldly.

'You're *that* perfect,' she sarcastically humoured him. But though he was joking, she knew he *was* about as perfect as it got.

'Apparently.' A teasing gleam lit his chocolate eyes. 'Though you and I know different.'

'True.'

'And what about what I could do for you?' he said softly.

'There's no redeeming me,' she said bluntly. 'And you

should be more careful. Reputations can only go down. Never up.'

'What did you do that's so bad?' His amusement told her he thought she was kidding.

He'd find out eventually. And no matter what she said in response, he wouldn't believe her. Nobody did. Not even her sister. And her father perpetuated it—not caring about the veracity of any of the stories spread over the Internet. 'Any publicity is good publicity' was his mantra. He was wrong.

It was only a matter of time until she saw the judgment enter James' eyes. Hell, she'd seen it last night. 'You took one look at me and thought I was trouble.'

'And I was right about that.' Softly, he didn't deny it. 'But haven't you heard? I like trouble.' He walked right up to her. 'I go out of my way to find it.'

'Only so you can fix it.' She glared up at him. 'And sorry, *Handsome*, I don't need fixing.'

'No?' he asked, so close she could feel the warmth of his body hitting her even through the baggy layers she wore. 'You need something else from me?'

She could hardly breathe for the heated tension in the room. 'All I need is a space in this bed to *sleep*. Nothing else.'

His gorgeously outrageous smile returned. 'Maybe.' He stepped to the side and then walked past her into the bathroom. 'But you might be surprised what I can come up with.'

She couldn't resist turning to watch him walk. Goaded by his jaw-dropping back view, she asked the worst possible question. 'You think you're irresistible?'

He glanced back from the bathroom door, his thumbs hooked into the waistband of his boxers, that wry-but-wicked smile on his lips. 'I guess we're about to find out.'

CHAPTER THREE

CAITLIN TURNED AWAY, hearing his laughter and the click as the bathroom door closed. He was being deliberately outrageous, trying to make her laugh and put her at a funny kind of ease.

She did feel somewhat better. At least they'd established an arrangement for the next few days. But oh, boy, was he a vastly different guy to the exhausted grouch who'd tried to boot her out of his bed last night. Still gorgeous, yes. Driven, yes. Determined—most definitely. But amusing, teasing, mercurial in his mood…not to mention arrogant. It all added up to appallingly attractive.

Still, Caitlin could resist anything, right? It was peace and quiet she was after really. She only had to get through a couple of nights next to him. Easy peasy.

She wasn't thinking of *being* easy.

She pulled her straggly ponytail free and found her comb in her bag. She sat cross-legged on the lower corner of the bed and worked out the knots before twisting her hair into a plait. She'd just finished when he emerged from the bathroom, a white towel around his waist. Once more Caitlin was stunned into silence at the sight of his shoulders, chest, and sheer lean strength. Not bodybuilder bulky, but not skinny. Just right. He winked outrageously at her before walking into the wardrobe and closing the door behind him.

A bare minute later he reappeared clad in a fresh grey tee and clean combat pants. She couldn't help grinning at what was so clearly his uniform. Clean-shaven, dressed, uber-alert, he'd switched on his inner action man.

'Now for the practicalities,' he said.

She drew her legs up and wrapped her arms around her knees. 'Practicalities?'

'Food.' He jerked his head to the side. 'There's not even a fridge in this place. We're going to have to forage.'

That easily he made her smile. 'In the wilds of New York city?'

'It's a challenge.' He nodded seriously. 'You up for it?'

Truthfully she'd been going to go with a container of yoghurt. She was on bread and cheese rations for this trip. But she needed to get out of here and inhale some fresh air. Cool the little inferno bubbling inside.

'Okay.' She swiftly twisted her plait into a flat bun—and then hid the lot under her black beanie, and grabbed her oversize sunglasses.

'What are you doing?' he asked, staring at her.

'Getting ready to go out.'

'You don't like the sun?'

'I don't like being seen.'

'You're used to being recognised?' His brows lifted again.

'It's unlikely here, but you never know.' There was always someone, and everyone had smartphones. A snap could go round the world in seconds. She'd suffered through that many scathing articles and online comments recently, she didn't feel safe from them yet—despite being in a whole other country.

'Why would people recognise you?'

She hesitated. Until a few weeks ago most people wouldn't have. It was years since she'd been on telly screens. But just over a month ago Dominic and his new girlfriend had set the hounds on her. Not that she was telling James about that mess. 'I have a famous sister.'

His frown deepened when she didn't elaborate. 'Well, if you don't want to be noticed—' he plucked the glasses from her nose '—you're going the wrong way about it.' He tugged the beanie off her head as well and tossed it onto the bed. 'There are plenty of blondes in this town. Even natural ones like you. No one will notice. But if they see someone so obviously trying to hide, *then* they're going to think you're someone worth snapping.' He walked into the wardrobe.

'Photographers linger in this area?' she called after him. She should have known it. This building filled with huge condos in central Manhattan meant serious wealth—no doubt celebrities were part of the body corporate.

'Sometimes.' He reappeared. 'Wear this.' He handed her a New York Yankees cap. 'It's not winter, you know.'

'Thanks.'

Fists on hips, he studied her intently as she pulled the cap down more securely. 'You really don't like the press?' he asked.

'Who does?'

'Lots of people want to have more than their fifteen minutes,' he said.

'They're welcome to have mine.' Caitlin walked out of the bedroom.

She'd actually had more than her fifteen minutes years ago, and she didn't want a second more. Which made the recent events all the more galling. Given she'd been out of the scene for so long, she'd forgotten how to play the game. She'd forgotten how much it hurt. And worse, both the field and her opponents of today were bigger and more vicious than before.

She lost her stomach in the elevator ride down to the lobby. Well, maybe it wasn't the elevator, maybe it was a weird combo of nerves and excitement and a fragile possibility of happiness. Outside she drew breath and blinked at the mid-morning sunlight. Could she really walk down the street like a free person?

The last few weeks in London she'd been a virtual prisoner, afraid not only of whether there'd be a photographer lurking, but the reaction of the general public. She'd dreaded anyone recognising her. Having been labelled the psycho ex of the 'hot young actor' and the woman who'd gone crazy in her attempts to get him back, she'd been on the receiving end of the venom. They said she'd gone stalker when Dominic broke up with her. That she'd used the possibility of a baby to try to get him back. That she'd terminated that pregnancy when he refused to come to heel.

Lies. Vicious, hurtful lies. Every one of them.

And of course those stories were accompanied by all the articles comparing her to her sister—a resurgence of the pieces penned years ago. She was proud of Hannah, pleased for her. But her success came at a cost to Caitlin. The press had polarised them way back when—the 'good sister' versus 'the bad sister', the 'talented' versus the 'try-hard', the 'consummate professional' versus the 'demanding diva'. While Hannah didn't buy into it, didn't add to the rumour mill, or perpetuate it, their father always had. He still was, with his apparent attempt to 'reach out' to Caitlin, his 'troubled younger daughter'. Through the press of course. As if what had been written were true.

She'd never forgive him for that.

She'd never wanted her life to become like some scripted reality TV show. Didn't hunger for fame the way her father did or have a passion for being on film like her sister. She'd worked as a child model and actress purely because she'd been told to. Because they'd needed the money. She'd got out of it as soon as she could—as soon as she'd forced them to drop her.

Now she just wanted to be left in peace to do her own thing.

Here, now, in New York, the streets were crowded with people busily going their own way, getting to where they needed to go and not paying attention to anyone else. Moving fast and free. She wanted to be like them.

'First time in Manhattan?' James' amused voice broke into her reverie.

She realised she was standing stock-still, staring at the crowds walking down the sidewalk. She tore her gaze away from the scene and looked up at him, pasting a smile to her lips. 'It's that obvious?'

His eyebrows flickered. 'What's first on the list?'

'The list?' She echoed like an idiot as she looked at him in the midday light. He really was extremely compelling— tall, focused, intriguing.

'Your "must-see, must-do" itinerary,' he explained.

'Oh.' She turned and fell into step with him. 'Do you know, I don't know. I haven't had the chance to figure it out.' She glanced up and saw his surprised expression. 'The trip was a last minute thing.'

'You must have some ideas. No?' He frowned. 'Come on, let's eat and I'll give you a rundown of the highlights.'

'The Wolfe Guide?'

'Something like that.' He led her a few more paces down the block and then turned, holding the door for her.

A diner like one out of an old Seinfeld episode? She grinned. Okay, she could do that. She was definitely in the Big Apple now.

He slid into a booth. She sank into the seat opposite and toyed with the menu.

'You ready to order?' a waitress asked.

Caitlin hesitated.

'I'll have blueberry pancakes, please,' James ordered, then looked at Caitlin and winked. 'Nothing beats dessert for brunch.'

She faux winced and ordered just a coffee.

'That's all you want?' He frowned as the waitress departed.

'It takes a while for my appetite to wake up,' she lied, fiddling with a sugar sachet to avoid looking at him. It wasn't an outrageously expensive place, but she was going to have to be careful.

'It should be awake by now,' he half snorted. 'It's after midday—we slept through breakfast and lunch.'

Well, her budget was more a one-meal-a-day deal, but she wasn't going to tell him all her sad little secrets.

'So, you must have some kind of list,' he said, sitting back as the waitress came and poured their coffees. 'Got to have the usual things…Statue of Liberty, Times Square, Rockefeller Center…'

'Yeah, I guess so.' She picked up her cup and blew on the coffee before stealing a quick sip.

An insulted expression crossed his face. 'Are you not fully excited about being in New York?'

She laughed and set down her cup. 'I am. Oh, I absolutely am.' But it hadn't struck her before that she'd be here seeing it on her own. And that she'd hardly be able to afford a thing. All she'd been thinking about was escaping. She was going to need a second to get her head around it.

And just like that it came—the surge of happiness. She was free. She might even have some fun. She was in Man-freaking-Hattan.

His pancakes arrived and he began decimating the huge tower with a remarkable speed. He glanced up and caught her amused expression.

'Brothers,' he explained out of the corner of his mouth. 'Eat it or lose it.'

'I'm not going to steal your lunch.'

His eyebrows lowered as he eyed the lonely cup in front of her. 'Maybe you should.'

'I'm not a fan of pancakes.'

The look he shot her then was of such pure disbelief she couldn't help chuckling. Then she went for distraction. 'So aside from the Statue of Liberty, what do you recommend?'

He munched and thought about it for a bit. 'Depends.'

'On?'

'What you're into.' He speared through three pancakes at once. 'There's something for everyone in this city. So what are you into?'

'I don't know.'

He paused and met her eyes. 'You don't know what you're into? What you want?'

She felt that wretched heat bloom in her cheeks. Why must she read innuendo into everything the man said? 'I just want to see some things.'

'Not *do* some things?'

Oh, there was innuendo there. 'Perhaps.'

'You're going to need more than coffee if you're planning on doing things.'

'Then perhaps today I'll just stick with seeing.'

He inclined his head with a wry grin. 'Fair enough.'

She stiffened as he opened his wallet. 'You're not paying.'

'Yeah? Well, I don't expect you to buy me breakfast.' He sighed. 'Though would it be so bad to let me buy you a coffee to make up for my rudeness of last night?' He looked across at her for a moment, his eyebrows lifting higher as the seconds passed. 'Clearly it would.'

Caitlin swallowed the last mouthful of her coffee. She

was an idiot. Overreacting because she was oversensitive. The events of the last six weeks had made her paranoid. She wasn't being fair. It was one thing not to trust, but to treat someone rudely? 'I'm sorry, it was me being rude then. I really appreciate the way you're helping me out.'

He met her gaze; a low smile spread across his face. An open, nothing-held-back smile that flooded her with warmth. 'No problem.'

She stood, trying to escape the megawatt impact of that smile. 'Thanks.'

Two minutes later James dug his mobile out and switched it on, keeping an eye on his new roommate as she walked off down the street ahead of him.

She'd finally smiled, finally relaxed and accepted the situation. And his apology. Good. Now all he had to do was get out of here as soon as possible. The condo was hers. The sooner he got back on a plane, the better.

With an effort he glanced at his phone. No messages. Most everyone thought he was in the back of beyond and wouldn't expect to hear from him. Except for his boss. He touched her name in his contacts list. True to all-efficient form she answered on the second ring.

'I need a project,' he said as soon as she'd said hello.

'You're only just back.'

'I know. And bored already,' he lied.

'Well, I do have something…' Lisbet trailed off.

Despite his lingering tiredness, his skin prickled. He did like to stay busy. 'Where?'

'Here.'

'Forget it.' He heard Lisbet's impatient mumble and hurried on. 'You know I don't want a desk job. Can't think of anything worse.'

'You have other skills we need. Not all our people can

perform the way you do in a public environment. Communication, fundraising is necessary.'

'I'm not your poster boy—you know this already.' He
watched as Caitlin disappeared into the throng walking
downtown. Fleetingly he hoped she'd be okay on her own—
that she'd not just 'see' but 'do'.

'And you know you already *are*. You could still go on
overseas projects,' said Lisbet. 'Just fewer.'

Lisbet had been on at him about taking on more of a
public role for a while now, but he wasn't giving up the real
work. He preferred to be an anonymous part of a team, not
a figurehead. 'Don't lessen my load,' he warned her. 'I'd
have to offer my services elsewhere.'

'All right,' she sighed. 'But I'm not going to stop trying
to change your mind.'

'Try all you like, but keep the field assignments coming.' He turned back towards the condo.

'There's no end to them,' she snorted. 'But *you* need at
least a fortnight off.'

A fortnight? He halted in horror, earning a muffled curse
from the pedestrian behind him who'd swerved to avoid
smacking into him. James waved a vague apology and then
frowned at the pavement.

No *way* could he share a bed with Caitlin for a fortnight. Not without asking for the improper. 'I don't need
that long,' he quickly said to Lisbet. 'I'm ready to ship out
again tomorrow.'

'No. I'm not letting you burn out,' she answered.

'Never going to happen.'

'That's what they all say, right before they crash,' she
said briskly. 'Go spend some time with your family. You've
been overseas for months.'

'I like being overseas.' He liked his family too, but he
liked being away and busy more.

He heard her sigh. 'If you insist on doing something, you can come to the charity gala on Thursday night. I'll put your name down now.'

Oh, hell, that was even *worse*. 'Lisbet, I don't—'

'It's only one night,' she wheedled. 'You can show me how refreshed you are so I'll send you back into the fray sooner.'

'Fine,' he snapped, letting her manipulate him—mainly because he knew rolling up to the event was part of his duty. He turned his phone off and shoved it into his back pocket.

Two weeks? What was he supposed to do with all that time? He hadn't had more than a few days off in years and that was the way he liked it. If he stayed in town more, his parents would put the pressure on about other—more personal—things. But they were going to have to save that for his brothers. James would never settle down. He'd seen how tragedy tore a family apart. He wasn't doing that to anyone else again. Definitely not having a wife or children of his own. He'd work for other people's families. That was how he got satisfaction and some semblance of peace. So he'd even help his unexpected roommate. His pain in the neck roommate. Pretty roommate. Sassy, sexy roommate…

Two weeks?

He yanked his wayward thoughts to a halt, frowning again. But he couldn't toss her out. There was a code—written by his own family in fact. *You welcomed, opened up, let the weary traveller rest.* How many times had he stayed at places where it must have been uncomfortable or awkward for the people who were hosting him? But they never said no. The basic kindness of people never failed to touch him. Yeah, the least he could do was offer the same in return. Kindness *without* strings. Certainly not sexual strings. He'd ice this edge he had for her. It was only re-action to circumstance anyway. He'd been working back-

to-back projects, had hardly seen a woman in any sexual
sense—only broken people in need of practical help. The
idea of sex hadn't entered his head in recent weeks. So of
course it had roared in on flaming wheels now he was in
the clear and confronted with a woman wearing little and
already in his bed.

The urge to cut loose sneakily called. He could charm
a *little*, couldn't he? Not everything in his life needed to
be that intense life-and-death stuff. He could coast along
with his lovely roommate for a few days until his boss let
him out on assignment again. A slight flirt wasn't going to
harm. And the amusement, the thrill he felt when Caitlin
hit back? He couldn't resist stirring that. He couldn't resist
the challenge of making her blush, smile, spark.

He walked back to the condo and spent the rest of the
afternoon talking through the refit plans with the design
team—tweaking here and there while he had the chance.
After they left he glanced at his watch. Where was Caitlin? Hours had passed since she'd left him outside the diner.
What tourist stuff had she soaked up? Had she eaten dinner? He waited, in case she hadn't. The evening progressed.
Nine o'clock came and went. So did ten.

Still no Caitlin.

Adrenalin tightened his muscles. Unable to ignore the
pleas from his stomach, or the urge to move in *some* way,
James headed out and picked up a pizza. He wandered round
the cold, empty floor of his lounge, eating and distracting
himself by imagining what it was going to look like once
the changes had been made.

The second hand on his watch ticked on. Still she didn't
return. Concern pressed. Had he scared her off? Had she
gone to stay somewhere else? Where? But she'd left her
small toiletries bag in the bathroom. So did that mean she
was lost—or something worse?

Hell. He tossed the uneaten crusts in the pizza box. Why was he so worried? She was grown-up. He wasn't her damn guardian. He forced himself to take a shower and go to bed. If he didn't get some sleep he'd look a wreck at the bloody gala and Lisbet would keep him chained to some desk for ever. But he didn't bother trying to sleep. He tried to read.

In reality, he waited.

Caitlin crept up the stairs, hyped about her day yet awkward about the upcoming sleep situation. Hopefully James was long asleep already. If so, she wouldn't wake him, given he slept like the dead. But as she climbed to the top floor she saw light emanating from the room. She swallowed back the surge of adrenalin and walked in.

Oh, where was the *mercy*? The man was in bed, apparently not wearing anything but the sheet covering his lower half. His bare, bronzed, muscled chest yanked her attention and sizzled her skin. She didn't know where to look. But she couldn't wipe the smile from her face.

'You had a good day?' He'd glanced up from the iPad he'd been reading.

'Amazing.' She bit her lip, wondering for a second if he'd been searching anything on the web. But his smile was still too warm and, frankly, the guy probably had way better things to do than bother finding out about her. It wasn't as if he were really interested, right?

'So you saw?' he asked, a teasing glint in his eye.

'I saw.' And man, was she *seeing* now.

'And did?'

'I saw more than did.' She glanced away, trying to re-count her day rather than drool. 'Times Square, Rockefeller Center—as you said. And tonight I saw a Broadway show, which was *so* awesome.' She beamed and looked back at him. 'That rocked. And now I'm really sore. My feet,' she explained as his brows lifted. 'I've walked miles.'

'Ah.' He nodded. 'So now you need rest.'

'Yeah.' That wretched heat beat its way into her cheeks. Somehow she couldn't think 'rest' when he was in bed like that—all big and bare and bold.

'You're going to sleep in the travel clothes?' he asked softly, a way too wicked whisper.

'I don't have much choice,' she said wryly.

'Wear another of my T-shirts.'

She licked her dry lips. 'I don't think the grey is my colour.' She tried to joke, because she knew he was joking with her like some panto character—all twirling moustache and gleaming eyes.

'I'm betting all colours would suit you,' he said.

'Are you flirting with me again?' She tried to stand tall. Tried to breathe. But the heat he generated burned her lungs.

'I was trying for more subtle this time,' he said. Humour laced his words but his triple-strength-espresso eyes were locked on hers. 'Is it working? I'm a little rusty.'

Caitlin couldn't tear her gaze from his. Couldn't contain her own rusty reply. 'Maybe you should try a little harder.'

He stilled; his alert eyes drilled as if he was searching out her secrets. That tiny roguish twist to his lips remained. 'How hard?'

She swallowed. But then shook her head, taking a step back from the ledge; she wasn't buying into this game. Because it *was* a game. 'I'm not sure you can deliver.'

'How do you know if you don't let me try?' His voice deepened; so did the amusement slipping into his eyes. 'I don't like not being given the opportunity to prove myself.'

She dragged in a scalding breath. 'This is you being brotherly?'

His smile broadened. His shoulders rose and fell in an easy gesture. 'You make it very difficult not to tease you.'

Caitlin sent him a look and stalked into the bathroom, locking the door on his low laughter. The man was *all* tease, with the lack of shirt and lapse into outrageous flirt. He was only doing it to amuse himself, she knew that, but it was fun and frankly a little flattering to her decimated-by-Dominic ego. So what if James didn't mean it?

Trouble was her body was *totally* buying it. All aware, totally absorbed by his physique. With that chest and those sculpted abs, all she wanted was to wrap herself around him. Her body was taking his carefree, fun flirt way too seriously. Good thing she was human and able to control her bodily desires.

Will power over want.

She towelled off and pondered her nightwear dilemma. One of his grey shirts was neatly folded and waiting on a shelf. She half laughed as she saw it, feeling a ridiculous glow at his thoughtfulness. He might have been teasing, but he'd remembered her no-luggage predicament and was genuinely happy to help.

So the real question was what to wear *beneath* the tee. She should have been just a smidge less frugal and bought some more knickers this afternoon. Except she'd already blown her daily budget. So now she washed out her undies and hung them over the bath to dry for tomorrow—refusing to wince. The man spent most of his time in emergency camps—he'd have seen worse than a pair of knickers drying over a rail. Fingers crossed her luggage would show up some time soon. For now she slipped into the T-shirt and checked in the mirror how low it fell. Almost to mid-thigh. He'd never know whether she had undies on or not. It wasn't a problem at all. Right?

Emerging from the bathroom, she stopped in the doorway and saw he'd created a Great Wall of Pillows in an engineering feat that NASA scientists would be proud of.

'Like the border?' He winked at her from where he stood on his side of the bed.

'Impressive.' She was *so* talking about the tower, not James in nothing but boxers. 'That's a very big…pile of pillows.'

His eyes danced. 'I did ship in some extra. But it should hold.' He rather awkwardly turned towards the bed and cleared his throat. 'According to my boss I'm not going on another assignment for a fortnight.'

'Oh.' A *fortnight*? 'So you're on holiday too, then,' she mumbled, her face scorching.

'Seems so.' He pulled back the sheet and slid beneath it.

'Nice.' She couldn't think what else to say. She was going to have to sleep next to him for the next *two* weeks? How was she going to survive? She was too close to combustion as it was.

Hideously self-conscious, she crept onto her side of the bed. The tower was so tall she'd be able to sit up and still not see him. But she was acutely aware of his closeness, the image of him all but naked was seared on her mind.

She carefully clambered between the cool sheets and told her hyperactive senses to chill too. A fair amount of trust was required to sleep in the same bed as someone, but she was *safe* with James Wolfe. She'd already spent one night with him. Sure, last night he'd been too exhausted to do anything even if he'd wanted to, but she figured that— despite the light'n'teasy flirt—he really didn't *want* to do anything. He was too honourable, way too much the hero, to make an inappropriate move.

And that was fine, right?

He switched off the light and plunged them into almost darkness. Energy buzzed in the room. Her sensual awareness grew super high. She totally regretted the no knickers. She was too nude—and growing too damp. She couldn't really blame the shower. *Get a grip, Caitlin.*

She could lie next to him and not think about sex. She could keep cool and in control of herself. She could try to remember to breathe.

'You had dinner before the theatre?' he asked from the other side of the pillow ranges.

Caitlin swallowed a gasp. 'Yes.'

At that moment, a prolonged gurgling sound rumbled round the deathly quiet room. Her stomach had just proved her a liar.

'You spent your daily budget on your theatre ticket, didn't you?' He chuckled.

She sighed. No point in trying to lie now. 'Yeah.' Not just today's budget, but tomorrow's too. And the next day's.

'So you're hungry.'

Yeah. She was. For a number of things.

She felt the mattress bounce as he suddenly moved. She heard rustling. Then a tearing sound—was that *foil*? Was he—?

She yanked her thoughts from the rampantly horny. Man, was she that wired, that turned on by his mere presence, that her brain had fried, thinking he was about to sate her *sexual* appetite? That he was undoing a—

'Here.'

In the dim light she saw his hand stretching over their pillow wall.

She reached out and took the small rectangular-shaped thing he was holding out. It was slightly warm, slightly soft. And as she drew it nearer to see what it was the scent told her. Her mouth watered.

'Chocolate?' She felt almost faint at the divine smell.

'I always have some with me. It has nuts in it, though—
that okay?'

The man was an angel. 'More than okay.' She nibbled
on a corner, savouring, resisting the urge to swallow it in
one gulp. 'So this is your secret stash? That's what you
keep by your bed?'

'Uh-huh. Good, right?'

He was so good. She slowly sucked the chocolate lump,
letting it melt over her tongue. She nearly moaned at the
sweet sensation.

She heard his low laughter and he dropped another, much
larger piece over the pillow wall.

No matter if he'd only ever been teasing, she was all his.
A man who provided the necessaries of life—a roof over
her head and chocolate after midnight? What more did a
woman need?

She refused to think of sex.

A couple of minutes later he spoke again. 'How bad is
your budget?'

Caitlin smiled wryly. No point in trying to hide the obvious. 'Pretty bad.'

Frankly she wasn't bothered this instant because she'd
seen that Broadway show tonight and she was staying in
this incredible location, less than an arm's reach from the
hottest guy she'd ever met. A guy who slept in little and
always carried chocolate with him—

'A month in New York with no money?' He summed
up her life.

'Yes, but that's okay,' she said doggedly. 'I have a roof
over my head. I have eyes.'

'So you can do your seeing.' James shook his head and
passed the rest of his chocolate over the pillows. Hell, he
wanted her to 'do' too. He wanted her to do *him*. And could
anyone blame him when she was in one of his T-shirts

again, all glowing from the shower with her long legs and sparkly eyes, full of smiles and simmering anticipation.

'You should sleep,' she said, sounding apologetic.

As if that were going to happen when she'd looked like that. Tired but flushed—*excited*. He listened to the soft sounds as she settled into the bed—so she was ready to snooze? At least she had a little something sweet in her stomach now.

Hell. He really wanted to lick the remaining taste of chocolate from her lips.

He drew a breath and held it as he tried to calm the riot inside his body. Good thing he'd built the pillows up so high, given the way his body was straining to attention. This was worse than he'd imagined it'd be. No way was he managing two weeks of this kind of torture. He'd phone Lisbet in the morning and insist on a placement somewhere—anywhere.

A few minutes later he heard Caitlin rustle again. Then again. Restless? As restless as he? He grinned in the darkness. He knew all about exciting days in foreign cities and sensorial overload. It took a while to relax, no matter how physically exhausted you were. You needed time to mentally unwind after such a stint of fierce sightseeing. The rustling sounded again.

'You can't sleep?' he asked.

'Sorry.' Her soft voice filled him with warmth. 'Am I keeping you awake? I can't stop thinking.'

Yeah, he knew how that felt too. And he knew a cure—a focus on physical pleasure. Even the most stressed person could find that mindless relief that came after physical completion. But it wasn't something he did when on assignment. A few of the guys did. Some of the things they saw when on task compelled a need to affirm life. Or find an escape. So they hooked up with nurses. Or maybe visited a local late-night lady. But some of those women the guys visited had no escape. They needed money desperately enough to do anything. Emotions were fraught. James thought it was easier, safer for all, to steer clear altogether. He encouraged his team to do the same.

But here he was. Home. Safe. And unable to think of anything but Caitlin and what he'd do to her the second he got the chance. He was out of control.

'Tell me about the show,' he almost begged her. Anything to stop the lusty images pelting through his mind.

'It was amazing. *Crystal Sugar.* You seen it?'

'No. Should I?'

'Hell, yes,' she answered fervently. 'It's incredible. I've never seen anything like it. Not even in London. The costumes were ah-may-zing.'

'Costumes?' He grinned and listened to her talk on. So she was a showgirl at heart? It certainly hadn't taken much to pop that cork and get her flowing. Good. It was a perfect neutral topic. Because he wasn't going to get personal. They were just sharing a sleeping space. Nothing more complicated than that. 'You wish you were up there onstage?'

'Oh, no.' She sounded appalled.

'Just a fan?' She seemed too enthralled for that.

There was a momentary pause. 'I really do like the costumes. That's what I studied. Costume design.'

'Wow.' She was a designer? 'That's great.' But it didn't quite seem right to him. She looked more suited to limelight than lurking in the wings. With those aquamarine eyes, the blonde hair, the camera-conscious sleek figure, she was the epitome of starlet-in-waiting. 'So that's what you want to do? You're not really a wannabe actress hoping to make it big here?'

'Never.' Oddly, her laugh verged on hysterical. 'No. I'm all for the costumes. I like the backstage stuff. I'd love to get a wardrobe technician job here.'

'And a wardrobe technician...?'

'Preserves the integrity of the costumes, keeps them pristine and looking the way the designer envisioned,' she answered.

'They don't stay pristine?' He half laughed.

'Not always, no,' she answered primly. 'The dances are energetic so sometimes things tear. And get sweaty.'

Ah. He really didn't want to think 'energetic' and 'sweaty' right now. Not when he'd only just mastered his own mind. For a nanosecond.

'They're really heavy,' she continued. 'And hot. And they take hours of work.'

Hot. Like him, then. 'You're fully into it.'

'That's what I want to do, yes. I've finished a design course in London. Now it's time to get the job.'

'But first you have this month in New York.' Spending all her money on seeing the shows and half starving in the process. He heard her draw in a deep breath and let it out in a sleepy sigh.

'Yes.'

He rubbed the heel of his hand hard over his forehead and told himself she was answering the comment he'd actually muttered aloud, not answered the question he ached to put to her. Now other questions pressed. How did she know George? Why had he offered her the use of the condo? Why was she so wary of the media? But the question bugging him most of all was whether he'd still taste that chocolate if he kissed her now.

He wanted to kiss her everywhere.

Yeah, the lustful thoughts hadn't gone far for long.

'Goodnight,' she murmured. 'Sleep tight.'

He wryly smiled in the darkness at her last sweet mumble. With temptation lying a mere breath away, sleep wasn't going to win in a hurry.

CHAPTER FOUR

An endless, high-pitched screech shattered the silence. Bleary-eyed, James squinted up at the ceiling, wondering what the hell the noise was. Then it dawned. A phone. A real phone. Who used a land-line these days?

On auto he reached a hand out to find it and encountered a lump of something soft. Then he remembered the pillows. The reason for the pillows.

Shit. He flinched. It was too early. Caitlin would still be asleep. *Should* still be asleep after her big day yesterday. He jerked over and fell off the bed in his haste. Damn. He'd been clinging to the edge for fear that while asleep he'd act out his dreams and desires and move too close to her. Blinking fast, he peered round the floor to find the phone. The thing was right underneath the bed. One of the builders must have plugged it in thinking he was being helpful. He snaked an arm and hauled the receiver off the hook and put it to his ear.

'Yes?' he bit out in a furious whisper.

'James?' George's surprised tones burst loud from the handset. 'I didn't think you were back for another couple of months.'

Well, that was obvious, given the appearance of Caitlin in his bed. But James fought to suppress the irritation. How could George know James was going to be back if James hadn't told him—didn't ever tell any of them? It was his own fault for being so crap at communication. 'It was a surprise to me too.' He pressed the receiver closer to his ear and lowered his voice yet more. 'I didn't know we loaned the condo out.' It was their private escape.

'You're not the only Wolfe who helps out people in trouble,' George answered.

James paused as his pulse did a quickstep. Then he couldn't resist asking, 'She's in trouble?'

'She's had a rough time. So be nice and don't make her life any harder than what it is.'

Harder than what? James gritted his teeth. He knew there was something up. He should have asked her more. 'Who is she? What happened?' He held his breath, aware she was only a few feet away and probably awake and listening to every word.

'Why don't you ask her? Actually talk to a person for a change.' George laughed, clearly missing the tension stringing out James. 'How are you both squeezing in there? I thought the refurb was going to take a few weeks.'

'Longer. But we're managing,' James hedged. 'I'm only here for a day or two. Where are you?'

'The cottage.'

At *home*? 'Really?' The knowledge kicked him under the ribs. His twin was back. With his family.

'Uh-huh. And Mum's coming. She's going to want to talk to you—'

'George, no, don't. Tell her I'm—'

'Tell her yourself.'

'Tell me what?' A third, distant, voice echoed along the line.

Damn. 'Hey, Mum.' James pressed his body into the rug and closed his eyes tight.

'James! You're in New York?' His mother sounded breathless in surprise. 'When are you coming to see us?'

There it was. No preamble. No niceties—no 'how was your trip'. It was straight into the expectation. The demand. And it was fair enough—she was his mum after all.

'It's been so long since we've seen you,' she added.

'It's been busy.' He gripped the handset tightly.

'But not now?'

'No, still busy. I'm only in town a couple of days. I'm not going to have time to—'

'Months, James. It's been months.' She spoke quietly.

He turned up to Thanksgiving, to Christmas, to his parents' birthdays. Couldn't that be enough? But it wasn't. He knew his absence bothered them. But he couldn't sit back and relax. He liked to stay busy. *Needed* to. James covered his closed eyes with his hand.

'Is a quick visit too much to ask?' his mother asked.

'I'm sorry,' James spoke briskly. 'I'm only in New York another day.'

'Oh.' There was a pause. Then she rallied. 'Where are you going next?'

'Uh.' He tried to think up something plausible. 'Conference in Northern Japan.'

'Japan? Nice.'

James winced at the disappointment his mother was trying so hard to hide. But if he showed up at home she'd only be more disappointed. Better to keep his visits quick, painless and rare. 'It should be interesting.'

'Maybe we'll see you when you get back.'

He could hear his mother trying to smile.

'Maybe,' he answered.

The line went dead. James banged the receiver down and cursed. He should never have picked the bloody thing up.

'Well, well,' a sultry voice commented slyly.

James lifted his hand from his eyes and looked up from his awkward position on the floor. She was peering over the edge of the mattress, looking down at him like the cat who'd got the cream.

'Who'd ever have thought that James Wolfe was capable of lying to his loved ones?' She inched forward so she hung a little further over the edge, a smile on her lips that spelled trouble. 'Only another *day* in New York? Last night you told me you were on holiday for two weeks.'

'I'm tired.' He shrugged. 'I don't want to spend more time travelling.'

'Diddums. First world problems.' Her blue eyes were too alert and all-seeing for this time of the morning.

'Have you got a problem with me?' He tried to brazen it out.

'Possibly. You're avoiding your family?'

He wanted to avoid that topic. 'What, you're saying you've never told a lie?'

'Sure I have.' She shrugged.

It was the smile that did it. He wanted it. Wanted to haul her close and kiss it from her. He lifted his hand and very gently touched her chin with his finger. 'But I can't?'

'You're the good guy, remember?' The colour of her eyes deepened, the black pupils swelling as she stared down at his.

'What is it that's so bad about you? You look good to me.' He slid his finger along the edge of her jaw.

'You're flirting again? More avoidance?'

'With you, it's too entertaining not to,' he muttered. 'It's amazing how little it takes to make you blush. For a supposed bad girl you embarrass easily.'

She was blushing now.

'It's a skill I picked up backstage at all those shows.'

'You're saying you fake it?' he scoffed. 'Darling, you

shouldn't be backstage, you should be front and centre. Right in the limelight.'

'I have greater talents elsewhere,' she said smugly. 'One can't turn one's back on one's gifts.'

'Elsewhere?' He laughed and shook his head. 'There's no beating you, is there?' He liked it. 'You have a come-back for everything.'

'I can do defence.'

'I'm getting that.' He slid his hand round to cup the back of her neck. One touch wasn't enough. 'Deflection, distraction. You've got all the d-words down pat.'

'Especially determination.'

He stretched up and wrapped his free hand around her upper arm. So she couldn't back away. Because he couldn't back away. Not from this. Not now. *He* needed the distraction and the defence.

'What about desire?' he asked roughly. 'You can do that too?'

Colour scorched her face again. 'Is that what you want?'

'It's all about want,' he murmured, slowly, carefully applying pressure to pull her closer towards the edge of the bed. Towards him. 'Isn't it?'

'I think we want different things,' she whispered.

'Not so different.' He pulled harder, until she slithered right off the mattress and onto him.

Caitlin gasped as she crashed down off the bed and landed in a sprawl right on top of him—arms and legs akimbo. He was harder than concrete. All his muscles were flexed.

Dear heaven.

She put her hands on the carpet either side of his head and levered herself up enough to look down into his face. The action pushed her pelvis harder against his. She gasped again as the rigid length of him pushed hard against her.

But now he had one hand on the small of her back, keeping her body pressed to his and his hand circling the back of her neck was strong—pushing her head back down. Pushing until her lips met his.

Given her gasp, her mouth was already parted. So was his. Hot, hungry, he lashed out with his tongue, claiming her with no hesitation.

She heard his low growl, was aware a strangled groan had sounded deep in her own throat. But there was no stopping, no talking. No breathing.

It was all kiss. And not gentle. Not tender. Just raw, rampant hunger.

His lips moved, wide and wicked, slicking over hers as he swept his tongue inside her mouth again and again as if he could never get enough of her taste. His fingers pushed up into her hair, clasping it. She liked the tight hold he had on her. She liked the unrestrained need emanating from him. She was aware part of him was unhappy, still moody from that phone call. So she knew he was using her.

But she didn't care. She was using him too. Because nothing had felt so good in so long. He'd lit a fire and in seconds it burned beyond her control. She soared towards it—the pleasure, the possible release. The sheer thrill of his touch and the way it made her feel.

Pure euphoria.

She was on him. All over him. She writhed, her hips restless and circling, eager to feel all his hard strength under all of her body. The kisses were chaotic. No smooth skill or seduction. It was hunger. Frantic, fast passion. One taste not enough. Nor two. Nor three. The chemistry was incredible—irresistible. She gripped his hair with both her hands, keeping him in place as much as he was her. Keeping her mouth sealed to his. She tangled her tongue round his as he slammed his hand on the small of her back again to keep her in place right over his heat. She couldn't stay still—she yearned. Ached for it all.

Her body readied in an instant. She was wet, hot, slippery as she rocked her hips in helpless abandon, seeking closer, complete contact. She spread her legs wider, so she could feel his strength between her sensitive upper thighs. His bare, hair-roughened skin heated her more.

She wanted. She wanted, wanted, wanted. She moaned as he kissed her. Moaned as she thought of the more to come. Moaned as it wasn't happening quick enough.

She wore the T-shirt, he wore the boxers. There wasn't another item of clothing between them. She wriggled to accommodate him, fitting into place to feel his blunt, hard erection pushing right where she desperately ached. She cursed the cotton covering him. If it weren't for that he could be inside her already. She burned for him to fill her, to propel her furiously towards release. His fingers slid down over the T-shirt, over her butt until he encountered the bare back of her thigh. She ground down harder on him in instinctive reaction. His fingers began to trail back up her leg, this time sliding under the tee. As he encountered the bare skin of her buttocks he groaned, his body flexing in automatic response—a powerful, passionate thrust that made her gasp even as he plundered her mouth with his tongue. For a long moment they lay locked—straining together, his tongue thrust deep, his blind cock seeking to drive deeper still, while she bore down on him, open and wet and willing.

He tore his mouth free. '*Hell.*' He grabbed her hips hard and pushed her up—away from him. 'Stop.'

Panting, she looked down at his gleaming body. What the hell was he on about? She was seconds from orgasm and she wanted that orgasm. Badly.

'Caitlin,' he grunted, his breathing rough and loud. 'I can't…'

His words came choppy; his fingers bit into her flesh. There was no mistaking the rigid determination on his face. He didn't want to do this. Didn't want her.

Of course he didn't.

Caitlin froze as if she'd plunged through a crack in an ice-covered lake.

'This is a bad idea,' he said. 'I wasn't going to let this happen. I told myself—' He stopped again and dropped his head on the floor. It clunked.

Oh, so what, it had been her fault? Instinctive defensive anger flared. He'd been the one to pull her onto him. He'd been the one all standing to attention already. But maybe it was just his morning glory she'd been making the most of? Maybe he woke every day with a super huge, hot erection and it had nothing to do with her at all?

Oh, hell. She knew that already. All he'd been doing was blowing off steam after that awkward phone call of his. There wasn't anything more than that to it.

'Don't beat yourself up about it.' Awkwardly, she scrambled to her feet and then scooted back over the bed, getting as far away from him as she could until she hit the mussed-up pile of pillows. She drew on an icy cloak of indifference and attempted to minimise. 'It was just a kiss, James.'

He sat up, his head popping up over the mattress. 'That wasn't just a kiss,' he said drily. 'What it was, was pretty damn…uh.' He shook his head a fraction. 'But it's been a while for me…'

Oh, please. She didn't want him to lie or make up excuses or be polite and let her down gently. If he didn't want her, he didn't want her. No problem.

But cold mortification seeped into her marrow. Because

she'd wanted him. And he knew just how much she'd wanted him—she'd been moaning non-stop.

'Yeah.' She nodded, acting up the amused 'it-was-nothing' scene. 'So your judgment is warped. Kissing anything with lips would be good for you.'

His mouth opened. Then closed. Then he laughed. He stood and to her immense relief yanked on the nearest T-shirt. Grey, of course. Then he looked at her again, his voice dropping into spoof depths. 'So, how was it for you?'

She shrugged, determined to sass her way through the embarrassment. 'Just a kiss. Not that great.'

'You *do* tell lies.' He laughed again. 'Defence.' He nodded. 'I've got it. But—' his expression went serious '—you know this shouldn't happen. Flirting is one thing, sleeping together another.'

They already were sleeping together. Properly sleeping in just the one—albeit luxury—room. That brought a wholly different kind of intimacy. She was getting to know more about him than she ever would if they'd just had a one-night stand. But she merely nodded.

'It wouldn't be right,' he said softly.

Wanting her wasn't right? How insulting was that? She itched to rebel, to retaliate. Or better still, prove a point—take him, make him...

She halted her crazy vixen thoughts. As if she *could* make him. What a joke. He'd just proven he had far greater will power than she did. And hadn't she grown out of brattish behaviour? No more being Caitlin 'always wants more' Moore.

But that didn't stop her annoyance with his 'perfection'.

'And you always do the right thing?' she jeered softly.

A strange expression crossed his face—he looked almost wistful. 'Like most people, I try.'

Silently she stared at him, trying to figure out how the

hell to extricate herself from this nightmare with just a shred of dignity intact. To her relief, her mobile phone rang. She pounced on it, ruefully wishing it had rung five minutes earlier and saved her from the humiliation of all but begging him to screw her.

She turned her back on him as she breathlessly answered. She had to get the caller to repeat everything until she understood what the woman was saying. She still refused to turn and face him after hanging up.

'They've finally found my bag,' she said crisply, though he'd have got that from hearing her end of the conversation.

'Great. They're sending it over?'

She nodded. This was good. There'd be no more sharing of clothes. No more bare skin at night. And she wouldn't have to spend money she didn't have. 'I'm going to get dressed.'

She stalked into the bathroom, locking the door and flicking the shower to cold. She lifted her burning face into the frigid stream. Wished *she* were frigid. Instead she'd been writhing all over him—ready to orgasm within ten seconds of snogging. What must he think of her?

She grimaced. No worse than what he already had once thought—that she was a tart who'd sleep with anything.

She soon had enough of the ice water treatment and turned on the heat. She stood in the shower for ages, refusing to worry that James might need to use the room too. She was hoping he'd have left the apartment by the time she deigned to leave the shower.

When she did finally open the bathroom door and peer out, she saw the bed was now neatly made and—joy of joys—her small suitcase sitting on the lower corner. The airline lady hadn't been kidding when she'd said they'd already sent it right over.

She grabbed the case and darted back into the bathroom,

changing into one of her favourite floral dresses. Nice-fitting clothes were as good as iron armour. She brushed her hair and lifted her chin at her reflection. She could face him and not flush. No problem.

But he wasn't in the bedroom when she walked out into it. She went downstairs, listening hard but hearing nothing. She sniffed, slightly miffed that he'd gone. Then she sniffed again. She could smell something *amazing*. She got to the lower floor and stopped and stared. He'd set up some kind of camp kitchen down in the stripped-back, barren room? And even better, he'd cooked up something mouth-watering—that he was now eating.

He glanced at her and swallowed his mouthful with a muffled choking sound. 'I like those clothes much better.' He breathed in deep.

'I'm supposed to be flattered?' She locked into safe sarcastic mode.

'If you want my delicious breakfast, yes.' He retaliated by zooming back to flirt zone. And smiling.

Which was so brutally unfair of him.

'Then I'm flattered.' She bestowed a saccharine smile on him. 'Thank you, kind sir.' It wasn't a total lie; she was a little pleased—this dress had been one of the first she'd designed herself when she'd been playing about. But she wasn't letting him win any real points.

He continued to smile right back at her—his gaze warm and lingering. She clamped down on the warmth working its way through her. Did he really think he could charm them through this embarrassment?

'I'm sorry about before,' he said easily, clearly thinking exactly that. 'Maybe it was inevitable with two single people staying in such close quarters. It needed to happen. But now we've broken that tension, right?'

Oh, it so hadn't *needed* to happen. And as for break-

ing the tension? It had left her yearning for more. Hell,
her nerves were screaming at her to jump him this second.
As far as she was concerned, the tension was way worse.
'Yeah, well, guess we're just two little animals who can't
resist basic instinct.'

'But we can. We just have.'

And they'd continue to? No giving in to the searing temptation? 'Of course,' she replied through gritted teeth.

James turned back to the small grill and took another
pace away from her to get some very necessary space for
the gas ring. And himself. But she stepped after him again,
wide-eyed at the prep work he'd done yesterday before she'd
got home.

'You didn't want to go to your diner?' she muttered.

He gave her a feeble grin. He'd go to the diner in a heartbeat. But he knew she wouldn't. A coffee wasn't enough. It
was economics—he'd already known it before her confes-
sion of last night. He cracked an egg into the pan. 'I like a
home-cooked breakfast.'

Hard boiled, over easy, sunny side up, runny yolk...
He liked it all ways. Lots of ways. Just lots of it. Ugh. He
winced at himself and the deep, single, smutty groove his
mind was stuck in.

Treat her like the sister he'd never had. That was the
only way to get through. He'd think of her as a sister. Put
her firmly in the 'untouchable' basket. She needed a break
away and apparently had nowhere else to go. George had
said she'd had a hard time. She might make herself out to
be a tough nut, but James wasn't messing round with her.
And he did only ever mess about.

Except she'd gotten him so hot he'd almost come without
even penetrating her. It was pathetic. No way could he have
lasted even a few seconds more. He'd been rough, ready to
slam inside her the second he'd touched her, and would have

come the next second if they'd kept kissing. Worse than a youth fumbling through his first time. He wasn't doing that to her or any woman.

He blanked out the tiny voice telling him that she'd liked it. That she'd wanted it. That she'd been close to coming herself given the way she'd been riding him. And that he'd have gotten hard again in record time.

He burned inside. There was no getting away from it. He wanted sex. Couldn't stop thinking about it. These last few months were the longest he'd gone without all his adult life. It wasn't that he was a player, but he had flings. One nighters here and there. Until the last few months when he'd been back-to-back working.

He'd fixated on Caitlin because of her proximity, right? So there was the scene, the bars and clubs. Plenty of places to find another woman with come-hither eyes and soft lips who'd let him lose himself for a few hours. Except there was no losing 'James Wolfe'. His face had been plastered over the cover of the world's leading current affairs magazine. That image was everywhere over the Internet.

And way more crucially, there was only the one image in his mind now—Caitlin's blonde hair draping over the pillow, over *him* the way it had before. Caitlin's lips, Caitlin's eyes, Caitlin's curvy body. The desire for her had taken root and he couldn't get rid of it. He ached to pull her beneath him and pin her to the bed. He wanted to take advantage and tame that subversive spirit, that spark within her. He'd tussle and torment her until she was silenced and sated and looking at him with nothing but appreciative pleasure in her eyes.

He wanted her to look at him as if he were her sex-god hero. How tragic was that? Given he hated anyone else looking at him that way.

But the way she'd kissed him—hungry, passionate,

raw—had heated him alarmingly quickly. Too quickly. He snorted as he flipped her eggs. He'd hardly been a sex god this morning.

George's warning rang again in his ears. If she'd had a rough time then she didn't need him complicating things for her. He shouldn't ask. Shouldn't delve. She just wanted her little sightseeing holiday.

So what he should do was pack his bag and leave before temptation grew too great. He served up the eggs together with the mushrooms and tomatoes he'd cooked onto one of his camp plates. Holding it, he turned to offer it to her.

One last look into those blue eyes?

He was doomed.

CHAPTER FIVE

LEANING AGAINST THE WALL, Caitlin took the plate James offered with a cautious smile. He looked uncomfortably intense. He didn't resume eating his own meal, leaving his plate to the side of the small camp cooker—next to his iPad. But he didn't look at that either. He only looked at her.

'Tell me,' he said.

She paused, her fork partway lifted, her mind still on the electronic gadget. Had he been searching? 'Tell you what?'

'Everything. Why are you here? What is it you've run from? Why did my brother say you could stay here? How do you even know him?'

She lowered her fork. 'Why do you want to know?'

'Why do you think?'

She rolled her eyes. Didn't he get that she refused to dance that dance? If he wanted to know, he could explain why or find out for himself. 'Look it up on the Internet.' She pointedly looked back at the iPad.

'I'd rather hear it from you,' he countered.

Had he really not looked already? Or was this some kind of test?

She forked some egg into her mouth and took her time chewing. The guy could cook, she'd say that for him. She had another mouthful because it was so damn good. He stepped alongside her, leaning a shoulder against the wall so he was at right angles to her. Surveying her with that teasing smile on his lips. Clearly waiting.

He'd be waiting a while.

But her taste buds suddenly went on strike, her appetite kicking the bucket too. She struggled to swallow her latest mouthful. What was it he wanted to hear? Would he actually *listen* or would he leap to conclusions? And if she did tell him the truth, would he believe her? People tended not to. People tended to think the worst.

Maybe telling him would clear the sultriness of the air between them. He'd end this flirtation. He certainly wouldn't want to kiss her again. Wouldn't that make her life easier? Wouldn't that stop *her* stupid yearnings?

'Okay.' She put her plate down on the floor and reached out for the iPad.

He grabbed her arm to stop her.

'*Tell* me.' He frowned.

'Think school,' she said crisply. 'Show *and* tell.'

He released her and she took the device, switching it on and plugging in a search. In a second she'd pulled an old promo pic for her show. She turned the iPad so he could see the screen.

He took a second to find her in the centre of the group of youths and read the advertisement. His jaw fell open. 'You were a teen soap star?'

'Never a *star*,' she corrected with a wry smile. 'More notorious.'

'You told me you don't want to act.'

'I don't. I'm hopeless at it.'

'But you were—'

'In a British school drama for a couple of seasons, yes. Before then I'd mainly done ads, modelling work and stuff.'

'As a child?'

She nodded.

'*Why?*' He looked as if he couldn't think of anything worse. He wasn't far wrong.

'My dad was an actor. At holiday parks, cruise ships, panto, a few walk-ons in the West End. You name it, he did it. Then he got a few bit parts on TV shows. One episode appearances in "character" things. He wanted us to do the same.'

'Your mother?'

'Died when I was seven,' she said. 'We needed money and there was good money in TV. I did some child modelling, had that cute factor. Did a lot of clothing catalogues. Then I did some stage stuff and eventually I landed the part on the show.'

'But you said your sister is famous.'

'She is.' Caitlin braced herself. 'My sister is Hannah Moore.'

His brows lifted. 'The movie actress?'

Caitlin nodded, waited for it.

He frowned. 'She doesn't look anything like you.'

Bingo.

Hannah was brunette to Caitlin's blonde. Was taller, coltish, had darker eyes, bigger lips. Caitlin had been the stereotypically 'pretty' one with the blue eyes and the blonde hair. Hannah was more 'different' looking. Now she'd gone raven she was even more striking.

'So how come you're afraid of being recognised?' His eyes narrowed. 'What happened?'

'What happened?' She stared down at the pretty young blonde smiling out from the centre of the posed photo. 'I was young and stupid and spoiled.'

Silently he waited.

With an impatient growl she confessed. 'I come from this "luvvie" family. We grew up backstage. The modelling work paid bills but it was assumed we'd act eventually. I had basic technique but no real talent. But I got on the show and it turned to custard.' She frowned. 'I'd always worked, right from when I can remember. And yeah, I might have been spoiled but I'd worked hard. But I knew it wasn't my strength. I didn't really want to do it but I couldn't say that. So I acted out. And I was stupid. So stupid. I partied, I talked back...'

'You were the wild child.'

'And my off-screen dramas elevated our name.' She winced. 'I couldn't live up to it. The expectation, the pressure was huge. And there was no getting away from it. But my mistakes were my own. There's no one to blame but me. I earned myself this diva-bitch label and it got fixed with perma-glue. And like all good stories mine were embroidered—some elements magnified. Some just plain made up. I wasn't as bad as it began to appear.'

'So what happened?'

'I got fired, of course. I think, all along, that's what I'd wanted. I haven't been on stage or on a TV show since. Six years. That's for ever in telly time.' She'd escaped and gone to study. It was only recently that she'd been dragged back under. She wrinkled her nose. 'Except for repeats. They like to repeat some episodes.' She grimaced.

'Where was your father?'

Right in the centre. 'He was my manager.' Her father had let her down. He'd never stepped in to stop her. Never defended her. 'That's how it all started. With me. Hannah had always wanted to act—was dying to. But she'd not got any jobs. Instead I got them. It was the cute little blonde girl thing,' she said cynically. 'Eventually Hannah did a piece in an indie film. Wasn't even paid for it. But she got spotted. They finally realised her talent. And she flew from there.'

'And what did you do?'

'Stuck on the show for another season. Hated it and got worse in terms of behaviour.'

'Why didn't you just quit?'

'I couldn't. We needed the money. Hannah hadn't quite hit the jackpot then, she was a slow build before becoming an overnight sensation—that's the way these things really work. I brought in regular money that we needed. So you can imagine how mad Dad was when they finally called time on me.'

She'd lost all worth. All her value. He'd turned to Hannah. Helped Hannah. She supposed he'd had to.

'But by then Hannah was hitting her stride?'

Caitlin nodded. 'She has that quirkiness that the camera loves. There's no mistaking her for anyone else. She's passionate about acting. It's absolutely her thing and she is incredibly good at it. She disappears for weeks when she's right into a part.'

'You're close?'

Caitlin hesitated. 'She's very busy and I'm working on a new phase in my life.' She read the disapproval in his eyes. 'We really didn't spend that much time together as kids. But she's a darling,' she rushed to add. 'She deserves all her success. And she doesn't need to be dragged down by me. It was because Hannah knows George that I got the loan of this place. She is supportive of me. But I think it's better to keep some kind of distance.'

'You've shut her out?'

'No,' she said defensively. 'I just don't think she needs to have my affairs thrust in her face. She doesn't need to have her publicist deflecting questions about me. She needs to concentrate on her career and not have me as the sideshow.'

'But that leaves you alone.' He looked at her. 'Because I'm guessing you and your dad aren't close.'

'He's very busy too. He's still Hannah's manager,' Caitlin said softly. 'She has a whole team these days, but he's still very involved. And that's fine. I'm a big girl. I don't need a manager. I'm loving being in New York and being anonymous.' She glared at him, hating how exposed she felt right this instant in the face of his inscrutability. She didn't want to go any further—not into the nightmare of the last few months and the real reason she'd had to run. 'Anyway, you can't talk. You've shut out your family.'

'I haven't shut them out.' His smile went fixed.

'Really? When you won't even go and see them in the few days you have back in the country?'

'You think they'd want to see me when I'm tired and grumpy?' The smile disappeared altogether.

'Would it be so bad if they saw you tired and grumpy? Or is your image too important to maintain?'

'I don't care about my image.'

'No? So you have no problem with having that picture of you being sent around the world?'

'Okay,' he conceded with a sigh. 'I hate that picture.'

'Why?' Didn't he feel some kind of pride that he'd been able to help that girl?

He shook his head. 'I work as part of a *team*. No one person is a hero. We need each other. We're there to do a job but we have each other's backs. There's no room for egos. We all do what we have to do. It's never down to one person.'

Sometimes it was. He was the one who'd found that girl and pulled her free. Sure, maybe others in his team had found others as well, but for that one little girl James Wolfe was her lone hero.

'Are your colleagues bothered by the attention you receive?' Was that where his 'reluctant hero' mode sprang from?

He stepped back, his bottomless eyes fixed on her. 'There was some ribbing. But no, I know they'd rather it were me than them. In many ways it was great—it raised the profile of the organisation and that helps with fundraising and stuff.' He shrugged.

It was clearly a line from the publicists that he'd repeated a hundred or more times. 'And it's only having your picture taken. It's not that awful.'

Sure, against the backdrop of things he must have seen, it wasn't, but he couldn't deny the impact on him personally. She wanted him to acknowledge it. 'But it changes your life.'

'Again,' he noted, 'it's nothing compared to what some people go through.'

'You're being heroic again.' She chuckled. 'But you don't like it.'

'No.'

'It's so awful to be admired? To be adored?' She'd far rather that than be thought of as the wicked witch.

'People see what they want to see. But it's not real. They don't see through that image.'

His words pierced her defence. They were words she'd say and mean. But she couldn't believe *he* really meant then. That he could possibly understand. So she teased. 'Maybe you don't let them.'

He chuckled. 'Do you try to let them see through *your* image? Do you try to change what they think?'

She waved a hand as if brushing off the idea. 'People have this thing about leopards and spots.'

'So once bad, always bad?' He leaned forward, coming too close again.

'Angels can fall from grace, though, so you better be careful,' she whispered.

He didn't laugh, didn't pull away as she expected him to. As she was warning him to.

'I'm not afraid of what people think about me,' he said.

'Really?' She turned, tapped the iPad back to life and entered his name in the search box.

'You're Googling me? Right now?' he asked, sounding somewhat stunned.

'Why not? I get the feeling there's something you're not telling me. What else is it you're hiding from?'

Something flickered in his eyes before he looked down so she couldn't see into them.

'Search away.'

His careless drawl spurred her. To find something wicked about the so-perfect one? She wished.

In a second she had a spate of webpages listed. A number of links to one article in particular. The one that had come first in the search rankings.

She clicked on it.

Dated a few months ago, the article was illustrated with that iconic image from the flood-ravaged South American village. There was another, smaller picture of him walking along the pavement outside his local coffee shop. In the grey tee, of course, but with jeans this time.

There was a fact box about his family—the wealth, the travel bug they all had—briefly profiling his two brothers as well, labelling the three 'the Wolves of Manhattan'. Then the main thrust of the article caught her attention. A tabloid piece from a gossip site, the main 'source' was a woman who couldn't contain her enthusiasm for James.

My Night With The Scarred Hero.
  ...He's as generous in bed as he is in his rescue missions. A strong, loving partner who gives a woman his all... He's so fit I could hardly keep up. He had me seven times in the one night, I've never known a man to have such stamina. He didn't seem to want to sleep at all...

Oh my. Caitlin looked up to gauge his reaction.

'It's embarrassing,' he muttered. 'Fiction.'

Determined to stifle her smile, she tapped her fingers on the edge of the iPad and surveyed him. 'So she's making up how great you are in bed?'

'Well...' He laughed uneasily. 'It's just not something you want to see in print, you know.'

'Some guys would love that.' Most guys she could think of, in fact.

'I'm not some guy.' He frowned and then sighed. 'I was already...popular, if you like. I come from a wealthy family. I've got all my limbs...'

And he was so hot it was unreal. Plus he was clever, and a good conversationalist. He knew how to look at a woman. Then there was that edge. She'd seen it that first night, caught glimpses of it since. The dangerous glint, the possibility of strength, determination—he was capable of taking charge. *Control*.

Heat washed over her. Inappropriate, devastating heat.

'Then with that picture. The rescue work...' He tailed off.

'You became a hero,' she finished, licking her lips to ease their dryness. 'Even more wanted.'

He nodded reluctantly, slowly. 'And then that woman—'

'Sold her story and the hot lover legend was born.'

He put his head in his hands and groaned.

Hard as she tried Caitlin couldn't quite feel sorry for him. Hard as she tried she couldn't stop her own arousal either. *Seven* times?

'Are you afraid you can't live up to it?' she provoked, forcing herself to laugh and keep it light. 'Don't worry, everyone knows all the stuff in the papers is made up. We all know the "seven times in one night" was a massive exaggeration.'

He glanced up, his expression smouldering. 'I just don't want any more stories in the papers.'

'So you don't trust anyone.' She got it now.

'Not one-night stands.'

'And you're not in town long enough to start a relationship.' She tried to slow her zinging pulse. He must be lonely. Must be hungry for it. 'Isn't there anyone in your team?' she asked. 'In the paramedic, disaster community?'

'No.' He shook his head, the heat in his eyes igniting. 'I really don't need you to be match-maker for me.'

'I'm not. I'm just analysing.' She flicked her tongue over her desert dry lips again. 'No wonder you couldn't resist kissing me. How long has it been?' She glanced at the date of the article again. 'Ten months?'

For a vital, virile man like him that must feel like for ever.

He stepped nearer as his voice came softer. 'That wasn't why I kissed you.'

'No?' She couldn't move. 'Why did you?'

'I wanted to. I want you.'

Heat burst in a fireball in her belly. 'You stopped,' she accused.

'Because it was the right thing to do at the time.'

'And you always do the right thing.' She remembered from earlier. 'Or you try to. Why do you try so hard?'

He didn't answer. Instead, with his gaze firmly locked on hers, he tugged the iPad from her fingers. 'What's good for the gander...' He trailed off.

'Don't,' she whispered. All sensual heat evaporated, leaving her cold, empty. Afraid.

'You might have gone off the rails when you were a teen soap star, but that was *years* ago,' he pointed out bluntly. 'That's not why you're here now. There's something else, right? Something more.'

She always wants Moore.

'Please don't,' she asked again.

'It's that bad?'

'Worse.'

'Like I can't look now,' he said wryly, tapping her name into the search engine.

Caitlin closed her eyes and silence commanded the room.

James looked at the massive number of hits. Most of them were UK based websites. There was a heap of images from years ago. And then some more recent. Much more recent. An online version of a UK tabloid had a number of recent articles. None of the headlines were good—*Could she be any Moore crazy?* ; *She always wants Moore* ; *Stop stalking me, I can't take any Moore!*

He clicked on the last. Skimmed the article then scrolled down to the comments. Unadulterated vitriol. And there'd be far worse on those unmoderated sites.

'They always like to find the ugliest pictures they can.' She spoke in a very small voice.

True. The accompanying picture didn't do her justice. How the hell they'd snapped her like that he didn't know. She was beautiful in real life. Elfin, ethereal—seemingly incapable of looking or acting the outright bitch this article claimed she was.

She'd gotten involved with an actor. Dominic. They'd dated for the best part of a year—she'd been studying. He'd been growing in popularity. Publicity.

He'd ended it. She'd taken it badly. Turned stalker—especially when Dominic began a new relationship right away with another woman. An actress.

According to this, Caitlin had told him she was pregnant. Tried to emotionally blackmail him back to her. Then, when things didn't go the way she wanted, when he didn't return to her, she'd aborted the baby. And in the court of public opinion, she'd been crucified.

James looked at her, needing to read her expression. To ask for her truth. What he saw pulled his chest tight.

She'd had a shiny inner glow when she'd first woken this morning, a teasing light and a definite bite. Now she'd paled. The spark in her eyes, her speech, her spirit—snuffed. He wanted it back. It was what he liked most about her.

'I hadn't been in the papers for years,' she said. 'And now it's not just the newspapers, is it? It's the Internet and Twitter and all those blogs with anonymous people who love to spout hate. They pulled up everything from the past. It's so much worse than it ever was. I thought I could handle it. I could back then. But now I can't. Now I…' Her voice trailed off.

'Is it true?' he asked quietly.

'Is what true?' she answered, some spirit returning. 'All of it? Part of it?' She lifted her shoulders. 'What does it matter what I answer?' She shook her head. 'Will you be able to believe me? Really believe me?'

'I have no reason not to.'

She tensed. 'Yet the first night we met you were thinking all kinds of charming things about me.'

'I was tired and…really tired. I wasn't in the best headspace. It wasn't *you* making me think that way, it was me.'

'People naturally think the worst. People naturally doubt.'

He shook his head. 'In my job I have to trust people instantly. I have to rely on strangers in the craziest of circumstances. And most of the time, they pull through for me. Actions. It's always in their actions.'

'So what do you think my actions say about me?'

He gazed at her, at the guarded look in her eyes, and the hope she couldn't quite hide. 'Your actions tell me that you've been really hurt. You've run away—come to hide and recover in private. But you're also yearning to start again—so you have determination. You have pride in your work. You want to do well. You're willing to put up with a difficult situation in order to be here—so you were very desperate to escape. Perhaps you're also desperate to succeed.'

She blinked suddenly. Her gaze dropping from his as her lashes fluttered a few times.

'Whether every word in this article is true?' He shook his head. 'I don't think it would be.'

She looked at him again, her pale blue eyes shining, beseeching. He suddenly felt how strongly she wanted to be believed. Yet she was filled with fear. And sadness. A fiery basic instinct roared within him—he wanted to protect, defend. Reassure.

'I've never been pregnant,' she whispered. 'Ever.'

His chest constricted. Ached. So did his throat. He nodded. 'Then why have they run with this? How did this even get printed?'

'Publicity, I guess. It made for a good storm. He came out as the poor, wronged guy.' She shook her head, casting away the wretched expression, her defensive quip returning. 'The crowd loves a villain. Everybody loves to have somebody to hate.'

James stared hard at her, trying to see the true source of her very real distress. 'Did he break your heart?'

'Only by not speaking out to say this wasn't true. He knows it's not true. He betrayed me by staying silent.'

No one had stood up for her. Not her sister. Not her father. She'd not even stood up for herself. She'd run away. Could he really blame her for that?

He glanced back down at the iPad and flicked back to

the search results. He clicked on a couple more. One catalogued her previous 'crimes'.

'Are they all untrue?' He read some of the accusations. 'Did you get so drunk at your sixteenth birthday party you vomited on the production assistant? Did you insist on having first pick of all the outfits you and your castmates were offered? Did you have an affair with the man who played your teacher in the show…?'

'Actually,' she interrupted with a guilty whisper, 'they're all true.'

He laughed a little. 'Oh, Caitlin.'

'Well, in fairness, the outfits thing was only because I was really getting into the costumes. I wanted to put the look together. But I didn't go about it the right way. I was young. Stupid. I admit to the mistakes I made. But you'll note it was *me*, the sixteen-year-old who seduced the older guy—according to those stories. Thank heavens he wasn't married. I'd have been slaughtered.'

'In reality he seduced you?'

'Honestly?' She thought about it. 'I think I was easy pickings. I think he knew which buttons to push.' She looked him in the eyes. 'The emotional ones, I mean.'

'Where was your father?'

A flash of sheer surprise flitted across her face. And then she laughed. 'Exactly.' She shrugged. 'Enter father figure, stage left.' She sobered, the sad expression returning. 'The worst thing was the writers caught a whiff of the rumours and then put it in the show. I was the schoolgirl with the crush on the teacher.'

Yeah, it really wasn't funny. 'Your father didn't refuse that storyline?'

Her mouth clamped for a moment. 'My father thinks there's no such thing as bad publicity. He was always more manager than parent. I don't need a manager any more.'

So that left her without a parent? He didn't know what he could say to make it any better for her. 'That sucks.'

She inclined her head and looked him straight in the eyes. 'You really believe me?'

Carefully he watched her expression—reading all that doubt there. 'Why wouldn't I?'

'Reputation is a dangerous thing.' She shifted her weight from one foot to the other. 'Mud sticks and all that.'

'No,' he murmured. 'Why really? Didn't you ever challenge them? Didn't you deny this crap this Dominic-guy spread?'

'There was no point. People will always think smoke means fire.'

'No,' he challenged her. 'Sometimes it's just smoke. Sometimes it's just there for someone to hide in. Like a stage set.'

She shook her head and the haunted look returned. She glanced down, running over the long list of offences detailed on the Internet. 'The underage clubbing thing is true, as is the underage drinking. But I never did drugs. Nor have I ever self-harmed.'

She hit the back arrow on the navigation bar, and scrolled back a few pages until that mortifying article about him featured.

'Look at it, the grand total of two stories on you are fabulous,' she said drily. 'While the thousands on me are awful. Being labelled a sex stud isn't anywhere near as bad as being labelled a narcissistic, deranged stalker.'

She paused as the picture of him carrying the child out from the landslide popped up. She was right, but he still hated that image—what it had brought for him. A moniker he didn't deserve. A supposedly 'heroic' status. Because in reality he couldn't be less of a hero. He'd destroyed a family, not saved one. Yeah, the *real* story of his life, the most relevant thing about him, had never been reported in any newspaper.

Caitlin looked at the way James was sullenly glaring at himself in that picture. He was cradling that poor kid so carefully, yet he'd had the look of a fighter on his face— sheer determination as he ran. His T-shirt had been spattered with his own blood, pouring from the nasty-looking gash on the side of his head.

'Did it hurt?' *Ugh*. She clapped a hand over her mouth. 'I'm sorry. You must get asked that all the time.'

'It looked worse than it was.' He looked up at her, his moody reverie broken, amusement stealing back into his eyes. 'Some women are fascinated with the scar,' he said softly. 'They always want to kiss it. Like they could make it better with their life-giving lips or something.'

'And do those kisses make it better?'

He chuckled and shook his head. 'Truth? I lost most of the nerve endings around the wound. I can't even feel it if someone kisses it. It's sure as hell not sexy.'

'Roger that,' she said crisply. 'No scar kissing, then.'

Their eyes met. For a moment there was thick, expectant silence.

He lifted his finger and ran it down his scar. 'Women think this symbolises something that isn't real. I'm no hero.'

'You are,' she muttered. 'You're good.'

'Why do you think that?' That bleak, almost angry look returned. 'From what you've read?'

'From your *actions*,' she corrected. 'You're the guy who pulled back from having anything you'd like from me this morning.' She glared at him. 'Is it so *bad* to want me?'

He flinched. 'I was trying to do the right thing by you.'

'Who's to say I wanted the "right" thing?' She rolled her eyes. 'Don't you get it? I'm the bad girl who always wants to do the wrong thing.'

He hesitated. 'I wouldn't have said it was wrong. But it seemed to me you're a bit bruised and I didn't want to make things more difficult for you. Now I know for certain you are.'

'You cooled off to protect me?' she flashed. 'I can look after myself.'

'I'm sure you can,' he said peaceably.

That didn't soothe her irritation. 'And isn't the fact I've had a tough time all the more reason to do something decadent?'

His eyes sparked. 'Decadent?'

It would be *so* decadent. The guy was like that luscious, rich chocolate he'd fed her. The finest of ingredients, the smoothest texture, divine taste. Fit, strong…*seven* times?

He laughed softly as he looked at her. 'What are you thinking?'

'Very bad thoughts.'

'Tell me some.'

'You wouldn't understand.' She lifted her chin provocatively. 'You can't really be bad. It's not in you.'

'And you think you're the expert?'

'Rumour has it.'

'We both know you can't believe everything you read.' He pulled her towards him, his voice dropping. 'Tell me what you're thinking.'

Only a breath away from him, she couldn't resist. 'I'm thinking, everyone thinks I'm bad. Why not *be* bad?' She was tired of fighting it. Tired of trying to hold her head up in public. She wanted something for herself. Something fun. Something that felt good. And James Wolfe felt good. No one would ever know. He'd be as adamant on that as she. And she could live with that.

His hand slid across her shoulder, the tips of his fingers

seeking her collarbone. They were gentle, but firm. Hot. She tensed, trying to stop herself flaring out of control.

'Maybe it's not so bad if the world thinks I'm bad,' she added. 'Then I can get away with anything because people are already going to think the worst.'

'What's the "anything" you want to get away with?' His fingers moved south, tracing the neckline of her dress. Down towards the curves of her breasts.

She breathed quicker. Her lashes lifted. 'Corrupting. Claiming innocence. Taking someone over to the dark side.'

His eyes widened, then a small laugh escaped him. He shook his head slightly. 'You really think I'm good?'

'You better be.'

'Truth is, I can be very, very bad.' His fingers slipped beneath the fabric, delving towards her cleavage.

'So we should be bad together,' she whispered, placing her hand over his, pressing him closer. She ached to feel more of his skin. Less tease, more touch.

'Or good.' His finger traced the lace edge of her bra.

'In this instance?' she muttered. 'Same thing.'

He bent forward and nipped her lower lip. 'Let's both be very, very good at being very, very bad.'

CHAPTER SIX

CAITLIN MELTED INTO his arms—his kiss came quick and hard and she was so ready. Right here, right now. Just *right*. She groaned as James swept his tongue across her upper lip. She wanted him to go deeper but, to her stunned outrage, he pulled back and picked up his phone.

'You have an important call to make—*now*?' She scowled.

Amusement flashed on his face as he took another step back from her. 'Very important text.'

What? How could the guy even think? How could his hands even be steady enough to be able to tap out a text? She was wobbly all over. Needy. Hell, she had been for hours. She put her hands on her hips to hide it and tapped her foot to express her annoyance even more obviously. 'How is a text more important than…?'

'I'm ensuring no builders turn up here in an hour.' He grinned. 'In fact, I'm insisting no builders or workers of any kind enter the condo at all today.'

Oh. 'So you're putting up the "do not disturb" sign?' she clarified with a tilt of her chin.

'Absolutely.'

Well, for that the man might be rewarded. In a minute. 'Hmm.' She lifted her shoulders and let them fall in a careless shrug. 'You do your admin, then,' she taunted. 'I'm going upstairs to find my own…comfort.'

She walked oh-so-easily across the floor, head high, shoulders back…heart *thundering*.

But she heard his low laughter, heard the sound of confident, controlled movements. Footsteps fell heavy on the stairs only a few paces behind hers.

As she entered the immaculate bedroom he ran a hand from her shoulder down the length of her arm to her wrist. His fingers made a circle—a cuff—around her bones and then he tugged.

'Don't think you can turn your back on me now.' He spun her round and pushed her gently with his other hand, just below her ribs. 'It's my job to provide the comfort here.'

She fell back on the bed. He fell with her, his lips connecting with hers. She closed her eyes as she savoured the glorious weight of him. His tongue stroked deeper this time, seeking knowledge. She let him find it—opening up to let him explore completely. She lifted her hands, exploring the breadth of his back, feeling the strength of his lean muscles. Oh, yeah, the guy was fit. Taut. Hot.

But then he drew back, one hand pressed on the mattress beside her head as he levered away enough to look down at her. Caitlin stared at him through narrowed eyes. He damn well better not put the brakes on again. She'd do him an injury.

He stared down at her, a smile slowly crossing his lips. 'Tell me what you want.'

She let her hand fall. She was sprawled on a bed beneath him. Wasn't it obvious?

'Talented as I am, I don't do telepathy,' he said with a self-mocking grin. 'I don't read minds. And I don't like to make mistakes.'

'You've made mistakes with women before?'

'Some.' He nodded. 'So I think it's a good idea to clarify

exactly where we're going with this. I like my private life to remain exactly that. Private.' A vaguely uncomfortable expression flitted across his face. 'I'm a wealthy guy. I'm a little known. So I'm always going to get verbal consent. I'm always going to wear a condom.'

What, he thought she'd try to *trap* him? 'You want me to sign a contract and everything?'

He moved, his weight falling heavier on her so she couldn't escape and pretended to think about it for a moment, amusement lighting his eyes. 'It has possibilities.'

'You don't trust me.' Wasn't that a surprise?

He smiled, getting her annoyance and soothing it as he stroked the back of his fingers lightly down her neck. 'Actually, I'd trust you on many things. But I always ask that a woman doesn't kiss and tell.'

She rolled her eyes. 'You know you're okay with me there.'

'True.'

'I don't trust anyone about anything,' she said. She'd never have unprotected sex. Truthfully she'd not had sex in a long time. Which had made Dominic's accusations all the more hurtful.

'You want *me* to sign a contract?' he asked.

She stared at the wickedness lurking in his eyes. She understood he had little to give her. Only the one thing she wanted. 'I can handle a verbal.'

'What are your terms?' He lifted a hand, traced her features with a light, sensual finger.

Caitlin drew a breath at the sparks such a small touch ignited. And she went for it. 'Sex. Unlimited. No one else knows.'

'Unlimited?' His eyes kindled—darker, magnetic.

'As often, as much, as you like while you're in New York.'

She felt his muscles tighten, his erection pressed harder against her.

'What if you can't keep up?' he asked.

She didn't think that was likely. She'd never been so hot for a man.

'You're the one who has to keep up,' she answered back. 'I can just lie here if necessary.'

'You won't be just lying here.' His hungry gaze roamed over her features. 'Do you know what I haven't had in a really, really long time?' he asked.

She shook her head.

'Fun,' he answered. 'Simple, uncomplicated fun. Free and easy and filled with laughter.' He bent and brushed his lips over hers. 'Have you had that recently?'

'Hell no.' She half smiled. 'I don't want tortured and emotional,' she whispered. 'I don't want pretend promises. I just want fun, too. I want to explore and enjoy and taste and then let go.'

He lifted away again to watch her expression. 'Is "letting go" going to be a problem?'

'You think it would be?' she asked. 'What, you're worried I'm going to start pestering you for a relationship?'

He laughed at her horrified tone. 'Sometimes women like to look into the future. I'm more a one day at a time person.'

'I'm thinking one hour at a time,' she said baldly. 'No interest in thinking beyond that. So don't worry, no wedding-bell fantasies going on in this head. I don't want anything other than…' She hesitated.

'Sex.'

She nodded. 'I want an orgasm.' Several in fact. Enough to last her the year. She hadn't had an orgasm in ages.

He laughed.

'I'm serious,' she said. 'I'm still hot and bothered by that article. *Seven* times in one night? Was that for real?'

'You want to find out?' He shrugged. 'You want to use me?'

'Just for now.' She nodded, then looked at him slyly. 'You're not going to hurt *your* heart, are you?'

He shook his head.

Of course not. She smiled at him. This was good. The negotiations were done. Agreement reached. Now she could just enjoy. 'So we're having a holiday fling.'

'We are.' He smiled back.

She drew in a breath and released it slowly, luxuriating in the feeling of his body pressing against hers. But she didn't want to just feel it. She wanted to see it—taste, touch and hear his passion too.

In short, she wanted it all.

And if this was a holiday fling, if this was just their deal—with no one else knowing—then there was no reason to hold back from asking for everything that she wanted.

'It's been so long since I've openly looked at a guy's body and just appreciated it,' she confessed.

'You want to appreciate my body?' His brows lifted.

'Yes, please,' she said bluntly. 'I'd like to look at it. All of it. I want to sightsee.' She licked her lips as he suddenly rolled from her and then stood up on the mattress.

He towered above her, like a magnificent, living statue. 'You want to reveal it yourself, or want me to strip for you?'

'I'm quite liking the you stripping idea.' She coyly looked up at him and shimmied back to sit in a huddle on the pillows and give him space to move. 'How are your bad-boy stripper moves?'

'Have you ever been to a strip bar?'

She shook her head.

'But women like eye candy.' His smile was so devastating, so naughty. Who'd have thought he could do playboy so well?

She laughed. Then drew a breath as he took a step back and lifted one side of his T-shirt, teasing her with a flash of flesh. Anticipation surged through her.

He paused, angling his head in a total stud-man pose. 'If I do this for you, there'll be payback.'

Excitement burned deeper. 'What kind of payback?'

'Really bad behaviour,' he promised. 'Demands.'

He lifted his T-shirt again. She watched, unwilling and unable to speak. He pulled the thing over his head and carelessly tossed it to the side. Yeah, that was what she'd wanted, a chance to look her fill, freely and with all the time in the world. His chest was broad, sculpted, *real*. She could see the sheen of heat glistening on him, see the individual muscles flex and remain tense—strong.

Slowly she looked from his face, to his shoulders and then down to where muscles tapered to slim hips and the trousers slung low. The front of his combats was taut. His hands went to his waistband, undoing the button with a teasingly slow hand. Caitlin tensed. He was getting to the good bit. He unfastened the next button, then rolled down the waistband—exposing skin.

Oh my.

Caitlin was entranced.

And then he was naked. Commando man. Beautiful. A half-smile crossed his lips as he watched her avidly study him.

'You better get ready,' she murmured, rising to a seated position, so ready to pounce.

'Yes, ma'am.' He dropped to his knees and with a long hand he retrieved something from under the bed.

Oh my. She stifled a squirm as she watched him tear the wrapper.

'Brand-new box?' she asked, husky.

'Bought specially,' he confirmed, glancing up to send her a searing look. 'Don't think badly of me.'

'So long as you got more of that chocolate as well,' she drawled, 'I think you're a genius.'

He winked. 'Life's little essentials.'

He rolled the condom down, looking up to watch her face as he finished. 'You want me to touch you now?'

Oh, hell yes. 'I'm wondering what's taking you so long.' She *just* managed to maintain her totally fake air of sophisticated ease.

'Well, I was thinking we should take this slow.' Effortlessly he out-drawled her.

'Slow?' She gaped, with a start. She so didn't want slow. She wanted to rut right about now. She wanted every last inch of him to be locked inside her. He was *beautiful*—all male strength and humour and edge and she was finally going to get some pleasure. Something just for her. Something nice when she'd not had anything nice in months. So the last thing she wanted was slow. He was hers to look at, hers to ride…right?

'We have all day, all night and half the morning.' He laughed, roughly. 'I slide inside now and it'll be all over. It's been too long for me to hold on. I can't make it that good for you. Better to go slow now, so I can be sure you're satisfied before I—'

'You want to make sure I'm satisfied?' She flushed as heat poured through her. Did he not get she was a whisper away from orgasm?

'Uh-huh.' He nodded. 'I want to watch you come. Want to make you. Quick, hard, many, many times over.'

Oh, mercy. Even at his words she was rocking her hips,

wanting to be naked *now*. Grinning, he put his hands on her shoulders and pushed again so she fell back on the bed. Too slowly he unbuttoned her dress—every little button—until he spread the halves wide and stared down at her. She quivered as she saw the appreciation and intent in his eyes. Thank heavens she'd put on her matching lace and silk. His fingers fisted in the fabric of her dress. She lifted her hips, so he could pull it out from underneath her. Clad in only her bra and knickers, she waited as he looked again—and she watched the signs of appreciation—excitement—affect his body. Tighten. Tighten more.

'You're even more gorgeous than I imagined.' He ran his fingers up the inside of her thigh and bent to press a kiss along the path. 'When we kissed this morning, I nearly came.' His breath was hot on her skin, his words hotter. 'Hadn't done anything. You had me so loaded I had to stop before I embarrassed myself.'

'That was why you stopped?' She barely breathed.

Pleasure swamped her as he nodded, a sheepish look crossing his face.

'I wouldn't have minded.' She arched as his fingers teased nearer the leg line of her knickers. 'I'd have enjoyed it.'

'You'll enjoy this more.'

'My hero,' she cooed.

'You're going to pay for that.' He bent close, blew a small jet of warm air across her sex. She shivered, her inner muscles clenching.

Slowly he inched her briefs from her body. His fingers caressing still, his lips teasing every so often.

Not often enough.

Caitlin arched, uncontrollably seeking more.

'The thing I love most about the female body is its mystery.' He swept his hands back up her leg and then higher, across her belly and up to her breasts. 'All secret curves and damp spaces.' He licked his lips as he undid her bra strap and released her full, tight breasts.

'Mystery?' Caitlin was struggling to keep up with the conversation as he touched her with those too light, too teasing strokes—everywhere and yet not exactly where she needed. 'Are you telling me you have no clue?'

'What do you think?' His fingers slid right where she wanted them to go. His mouth followed.

With a muffled groan she closed her eyes, arching her neck, her spine, her feet, as excitement washed over her in a tight spasm. A delicious precursor to the release she knew could be so close.

Okay, he knew what he was doing.

He raised his head and switched up the rhythm. 'I mean I like to explore. It's a never-ending fascination. How best to arouse you... How else...and for how long...'

He'd only had to stand in front of her and she was aroused. Now she was burning. She arched her hips repeatedly, trying to get him to touch her again. There. Just as he had. She was *so* close. He teased her—knowing what she wanted. Giving her only half.

'I'm halfway there in my head already, you know,' she gasped, embarrassed at how wet and desperate she was. 'It's not all your doing.'

'No?' He laughed. 'Then I better work harder.'

No wonder he was good at his job. He put so much determined focus into the task at hand. His tongue moved in erotic circles. She wanted him inside her. That one teasing finger wasn't enough. He fastened his mouth over her clit and sucked. Adding to the onslaught by caressing the nub with the tip of his tongue. His hands clamped hard on her hips so she couldn't escape him. Her entire body tensed as orgasm approached. She heard the low sound of satisfaction deep in his throat as she shook in his arms—her legs spread wide, her hips bucking up to him. She cried out as sharp, piercing pleasure hit—quick and fierce and so, so good.

She slumped, panting roughly, trying to regain control of herself—so she could push for more. She wanted more.

Oh, she'd gone to heaven. This was intimate, raw and real...*honest*. And yet it was like a dream. A damn good one.

He swept his hands possessively over her lower belly, looking his fill at her slick, ready sex. Then he moved his gaze higher, to her heavy, tight breasts. He smiled and lightly stroked his fingers upwards, over her ribcage until he struck the soft flesh. He changed position, to cup her breasts carefully. Then slid his thumbs nearer and nearer her painfully tight nipples.

'Feeling better?' he asked.

She shook her head. 'I want you. All of you.' She wanted him inside her.

But he just grinned and started all over again with the slow teases—the strokes, kisses, licks, nips. Building her tension, making her *want*. Until at last she writhed on the bed, like a restless wanton, helpless to subdue the sensations clamouring through her body.

'How bad do you want it?' he murmured.

'As bad as you got.' She panted. Defiant. Teasing. Because she heard the tension in his roughened voice, she saw the steely grit in his eyes. The determination.

His grin quirked. His hands tightened around her wrists, preventing her from touching him. Preventing her from stopping him. Not that she had any thought of stopping him. He knelt above her, keeping his body out of reach of hers.

'What is it you want?' he asked.

'You. All of you. Now.' She was reduced to begging. 'Please.'

'Hmm.' He pretended to ponder her request. But slowly lowered himself nearer. *Almost* near enough.

'James.' She ground out his name. 'James, James, James.'

He pushed forward, slowly filling her.

'Hell,' he growled. An edge of desperation sharpened it; his grip on her wrists tightened. 'It's been a while, Goldilocks.'

'Ditto,' she breathed. 'And call me by my name.' Defiant to the end, she demanded he feel this as intensely as she.

He put on a puzzled face so she had to strain up and sharply nip his lip.

He laughed. 'Caitlin. Beautiful, fiery, funny Caitlin.'

He shifted, pushing a fraction deeper. He gritted his teeth.

She growled and lifted her legs to wrap them around his hips, pushing her heels on his butt to keep him close inside. So good. Too much. But she didn't want to lose a moment of it. Didn't want him to slide back even a millimetre. She strained her legs further around him, fiercely trying to clutch him closer. She moaned, wordless, unable to express how insanely good he felt filling her like this. He took every inch—and then some.

'You going to let me move?' he rasped as she locked even tighter around him.

She shook her head.

He chuckled, the tension in his face easing. 'Too bad for you.'

He, stronger than she, broke free of her hold. Withdrew. She gasped in disappointment. But then he slammed back into her and her groan came in ecstasy instead. He was hard, powerful, big. Now he thrust hard and fast. His hands still pinned her wrists so she couldn't touch him. The dominance merely turned her on more. She liked being at his mercy, enjoyed the power she'd allowed inside her. And she let him pleasure her from the inside out—met him with every stroke. Until, so quickly, she sighed, letting herself go in his delicious rhythm.

But then he stilled. Went slow, his movements teasingly uneven. His smile was almost malicious as he held her agonisingly on the precipice of orgasm.

'Don't you dare stop,' she growled at him.

His dark eyes pierced. 'I want to watch you come again. I want to feel you clenching around me. I want to soak in your wet heat.'

She gasped. His words alone heated her, but as he spoke he slowly rolled his hips, providing just enough friction to send her over.

Her neck arched and she squeezed her eyes shut as it hit. She cried out, her relief sounding raw, her fingers in tight fists, as spasms of delight shook through her. He stayed thrust deep inside, rocking in only the tiniest, most maddening way that maintained that pressure on her clit, so the sensations kept surging through her.

Oh, he was good. Too good.

She breathed fast, shallow, loud as she clawed her way back from the prolonged orgasm. Slowly she opened her eyes. It wasn't enough. She wanted it wild. She wanted *him* wild.

He looked it—with his face flushed, his eyes black, intent and trained on her, his jaw clamped shut. And his sex still slammed tight inside her.

'Satisfied?' she taunted breathlessly.

'Not nearly.' He bent and kissed her ferociously, his tongue circling in the cavern of her mouth. His invasion of her total.

Slowly he withdrew his cock, then thrust again. He lifted

his head fractionally so he could read her expression. She strained up to keep their lips in contact. She was building again already. So sensitive yet still aroused. Not completely satisfied because he'd not been satisfied. Another orgasm was yet possible. She wanted it. And she wanted it *with* him this time.

'Demanding,' he muttered.

He'd felt her body tighten on him.

'Is that a problem?'

His eyes narrowed, more determined. 'I like it.' He moved again. 'I like you.' He kissed her ear lobe, tracing the whorl with his tongue before whispering, 'I like being in you.'

She angled her head as he kissed and sucked his way down the side of her neck. Helplessly she rocked her hips beneath him, cradling his, aching for him to simply screw them both to smithereens.

'Show me how much,' she asked. 'Show me.'

This time he didn't stop. This time his breathing roughened along with his movements. This time he swore pithy and crude as he told her again how good she felt. How couldn't stop. How he wanted more. And he took more. Pushed for her absolute acceptance of him. Driving into her over and over and over.

She moaned with every thrust. Louder, harder, faster, like the animal she was. He was almost as loud, feral and grunting as he fought to fill her—and fill his own needs. His lips parted, almost in a snarl as the pleasure sucked her under again and she screamed.

He rammed into her deep and hard one last time, his body jerking, eyes closing as orgasm overtook him.

He slumped, almost smothering her. His harsh groan rang in her ears, but she revelled in his weight, in the thump of his heart against her breast, in his exhaustion. In the sweat pooling between them.

She smiled despite her swollen, oversensitive, kissed to glory lips. 'You know that only counts as one, right?'

CHAPTER SEVEN

CAITLIN MOANED AS she reluctantly woke. Her body tingled. He'd flipped her over for their tenth round only an hour ago, determined to prove that the woman's gushing in that article hadn't been a massive exaggeration and that he could, in fact, go much, much more.

'So how bad was it?' James asked teasingly.

With effort she rolled away from where she'd been burrowed against his side and smiled, happy to take the bait—and bite. 'I think you need a little more practice at being super bad.'

'More practice?' He lay face down in the centre of the bed, his words muffled by pillows and a delighted laziness in his voice.

She prised her eyelids open with her fingers. 'Much.'

He half laughed, mostly groaned. 'Tigress.'

She'd barely slept—she couldn't with the way he'd tended to her, tormented on her. The way he'd *touched* her... She was still floating in an utterly soothed, relaxed state. She'd never felt such freedom and yet such safety before. There were no morning after regrets here.

With a growl and a curse he levered up from the bed. 'I'm not looking at you.' He stumbled into the bathroom.

Caitlin closed her eyes again and stretched right out on the bed. Her aches began to ease; already she hungered for fulfilment again. With treatment like this, she could stay here for ever.

Her eyes flashed open at that wayward thought. Instantly, imperatively she reminded herself of some fundamental truths. Just as there was no such thing as love-at-first-sight, nor was there such a thing as love-at-first-screw. There was definitely no such thing as life-changing, earth-shattering, cataclysmic sex. So this dreamy, whole-other-plane of happiness she was coasting on was purely hormonal. Not actually *real*. Her pulse would settle, the softness inside would harden up again.

Dazed, she made herself drum up some emotional armour. Doubtless he had a million annoying habits—aside from the arrogance and occasional moodiness she'd already witnessed. And just because they were sexually compatible didn't mean they had anything more in common. The 'happy ever after' fantasy flash could disperse into the thin air from which it had come. It was a moment, that was all. Everyone knew the initial rush of lust faded from any relationship.

Not that this was a relationship.

Hell. Her mind was shredded.

This was just fun, easy sex. With the ground rules established and the end date already in sight, there was simply enjoyment to be had. Like having a regular booking at a fine restaurant, she'd be able to enjoy all the dishes over a few short days. Then end it satisfied, replete and with no ill effects after.

The bathroom door opened and he walked out. Rippling abs, massive muscles, even more massive erection.

Dear heaven. How could he possibly be hard again? 'Did you pop Viagra while you were in there?' She gaped, so tempted to climb aboard and take another ride to oblivion.

'Who needs that when I have you to look at?' he answered all husky voice, stubble and smoky eyes. 'You're the sexiest thing I've ever seen. And the way you move? The way you moan? They way you whisper sweet filth in my ear?' He shook his head and laughed. 'I can't *not* get hard for you.'

'You say the most charming things.' She shimmied into the sheets, wanting him to come back to bed. She'd discovered her inner nympho.

'I know.' He grinned.

But to her horror he walked into the wardrobe.

'Are you getting *dressed*?' she asked, amazed. How would he ever get his trousers done up? And what was with the hurry? Didn't he want to sleep? Didn't he want to put that fine erection to use?

She heard his bark of laughter.

'You're in New York,' he said. 'You should be making the most of your time here.'

'I am,' she called after him. 'I've already walked my own New York marathon. What more do I need?'

'You should be *experiencing* all the city has to offer, not just walking past all the attractions.'

'This is all your travel expertise coming out, huh?' She rolled her eyes. 'I'm *experiencing* local hospitality—getting to know one local very well. Isn't that enough?'

'No. There is so much to see and do. This is your holiday. And mine.'

She hesitated. Seriously? He didn't just want to have a holiday in bed? 'What did you have in mind?'

'Don't look so wary.' He waggled his index finger at her. 'It won't cost anything.'

She steadfastly met his gaze. 'There are different kinds of costs. Money is the least of my concerns.'

'Really?'

A small sigh escaped her. 'You still don't understand.

You had trouble over one news story, James. *One.* Do you have any idea how many headlines I've been in? None of them good.' She forced herself to get up off the bed and stalked towards the bathroom. The guy was never going to get it.

'You're still worried about being spotted?' He followed her, leaning against the doorframe. 'Well, so what if you are? Why give a damn? Why not just get out there and lift your chin high and screw them all?'

She kept her back to him as she turned on the shower. 'It's not that easy—as well you know.' She turned to face him. 'You're too scared to enter a new relationship for fear of the media finding out. Of someone letting you down.'

His mouth opened, shut, then opened again. 'That's not why I don't want a relationship.'

'No?'

'Of course it's not. I'm not that pathetic.'

He wasn't? She stepped into the shower. 'So why no relationship?'

He shrugged. 'It doesn't fit with my lifestyle. I'm away all the time. I'm never sure for how long or where I'm going to be going. It's not fair to ask someone to keep home fires burning.'

Oh, please, that was the line he was spinning? 'Military spouses do it all the time,' she said, lathering up the shower gel. 'SEALS go covert in all kinds of dangerous places, for who knows how long.'

'It's not going to work for me. I'm not going to ask someone to live their life like that for me. I'm not going to leave a family in the lurch if I happen not to come back. I'm not doing that to my kid.'

Raw vehemence tinged his voice, betraying emotion. A personal connection to the words? Who had he seen not come back?

She frowned as she rinsed off, wishing she were up close enough to see into his eyes. His family published the world's most popular independent travel guides. His grandfather had started it, his parents were also intrepid travellers. He and his brothers had grown up with the world at their feet. They were the ultimate success story. Living the American dream—independent, ambitious and happy, right?

'Maybe you wouldn't travel so much when you're settled. You'd take fewer risks,' she said.

His expression shuttered, he reached for a towel and held it out to her. 'I'm not changing my job for anyone. I'll never stop doing what I do. And I'd never be able to compromise it, not for anyone.'

Caitlin stepped out of the shower and wrapped the large towel around her. 'Work will always come first for you.' A little patch in her chest ached, but she got it.

His stance stiffened and he crossed his arms, regarding her steadily. 'I love my job. I need to—'

'It's okay.' She smiled peaceably, walking back into the bedroom. 'You don't have to justify it. I understand, I've seen it before. It's what you're driven to do.'

He regarded her, the defensiveness draining from his shoulders. 'Who else do you know like that?'

'My father. My sister.' She shrugged. Nothing but work mattered to them—for different reasons. Her father because he sought the fame and the fortune and he'd do almost anything to get it. Her sister simply because she loved it. She loved losing herself in a character, into someone else's life. Even better that the someone else wasn't even real. Work was everything to them, coming ahead of anything and any*one* else. Even family. That was the way it was.

Caitlin had thought she was okay with it. Over it. Until the Dominic mess. Until she'd been pilloried by the press and her family still hadn't stepped up to defend her. That had just ripped the scab off the old wound. Now she found it festered.

Now she would never put herself in that situation again. No relationship, no man was worth being second to anything else in his life—certainly not career. No matter how heroic he might be.

But curiosity mounted as Caitlin sorted through the clothes in her suitcase—why was James so driven? The guy had money, she knew that. Hell, he probably wouldn't have to work a day in his life if he didn't actually want to. So what made him want to so much?

'What led you into it,' she asked. 'You always wanted to be a doctor?'

'I guess.' He leaned against the wall, watching as she dressed. 'One of those games we all play as kids, right?'

'But why search and rescue specifically?'

'I did a stint in emergency field work as part of my training and it just fit. I knew that's what I wanted to do. I made sure that's what I did. All my training from then on was directed that way.'

His reply was so glib, she was sure it was the PR answer again. The one he'd given many times when all those people wanted his story after that landslide photo. If she searched on his iPad she'd probably find the quote almost verbatim in one of those articles spotlighting him. But it didn't seem to fully explain that deep drive—was there another reason he was compelled to work so much?

He walked up to her, suddenly turning her to face him.

'Let's go sightseeing.' He framed her face, tilting it so she couldn't look away from him. 'You can't hide—it's like you've let them put you in a prison. You shouldn't. You're not guilty.'

She shook her head. 'It's not that.'

He ran his hand down her spine, as if he were soothing

a spitting cat. 'Then what?' He drew her close so she leant against his body.

She didn't want to resist. How could she? But she might make him pay. 'Okay. I'll come out with you. But there can be no PDA.'

He tugged her hair so she lifted her face. He stared at her in disbelief. 'You're *that* paranoid?'

'The photographers might not know me. But they know *you*. You're like royalty here.'

She saw the denial flare in his eyes. 'You're worried about being photographed with me?'

She nodded.

He threw his head back and laughed. 'That's ridiculous.'

She put her palms on his chest and pushed, freeing herself. 'It is not.'

'It is.' He laughed again. 'But okay. If that's what it'll take, then no PDA. You want to walk five paces behind me as well?'

'Not a bad idea,' she said loftily. 'That way I can check out your butt.'

His eyes glittered wickedly. 'Come on. Come with me now and I'll let you do a lot more than check out my butt later.'

It wasn't quite five paces behind, but Caitlin did linger just a little as they walked outside the apartment building, purely to check out his mighty fine butt.

James walked up to the yellow taxi idling at the kerb. Tired but determined to do this for Caitlin. The right thing. She couldn't spend the next fortnight doing nothing but having sex with him. Much as he'd love exactly that. Except he knew he wouldn't—if he lay still too long, thoughts began to bug him.

He bent his head to look through the window and grinned

at the driver who'd picked him up from the airport only a couple of days before. Oddly, it felt like a lifetime ago. Life had changed. 'Thanks so much,' he said.

'Any time.'

'I might need you for a couple of days,' James warned.

'No problem. Where you want to go first?'

'I'll tell you in a minute.' James straightened and turned to find Caitlin. She was just in front of the entrance to the building, studiously—obviously—ogling him. He laughed. 'Come on, then, woman.' He winked.

'We're going by taxi?' She looked pretty damn happy at the sight of the yellow car.

'I massaged those sore feet of yours last night, remember?' James teased. 'I'm saving myself from the task tonight.'

She reached up on tiptoes and murmured in his ear. 'Maybe I'll require a massage anyway.'

Before he could wrap an arm around her waist and hussle her back home pronto, she stepped out of reach and opened the cab door, sliding inside.

James took a moment to inhale deep and tell himself he could manage the no-PDA thing. Climbing into the cab after her, he chuckled inwardly at her outrageous demands. The woman who'd been so tart and scathing that first night sure had a naughty streak. He loved it. Loved that she felt free enough with him to release it.

He knew she didn't usually. Hell, she was blushing now, even though she'd said her little vixen bit already. But it was because of the deal they'd struck—an unlimited, evanescent fling. It gave them both a kind of freedom.

'So where are we going?' She turned towards him as she asked, her eyes alert, face shining.

His tour-guide trick had been a damn good idea. The no PDA thing? Not so much.

James shifted on the seat and tried to convince himself that all good things came to those who waited. 'First we're going on a drive by. Edited highlights. So you get an overview of the island without destroying your feet. Let's start with a trip around the park.'

The taxi driver pulled out into the traffic.

'James.'

Uh-oh, he didn't like the edge in her voice. He glanced across and saw her gnawing the edge of her lip. 'Problem?'

She nodded. 'Money. Paying for this.'

He drew a breath and lied. 'The cab is free, right?' he called to the driver.

'Absolutely. I owe you,' he answered.

Good thing James had briefed him and already paid for the full day's driving.

James felt Caitlin's unrelenting gaze on him. To his astonishment he felt a flush mount in his own cheeks—probably deep enough to match hers.

Yeah, she knew it was a set-up. But she said nothing. James quickly leaned forward and pointed past her, out of her window. 'Look, you can just see the Chrysler through there.'

He knew distraction would get him only so far with her. He knew he was spoilt. It was pure luck he'd been born into an extremely wealthy family. Hell, he donated almost his entire salary to charity because he already had enough income from his trust fund. He didn't *need* to work a day in his life, not for money. But for sanity? For self-worth? For dignity? He'd work every hour he could. Usually he took care not to flash his funds around the guys he worked with. Certainly not around the people who'd more often than not just lost everything.

But he wanted to take Caitlin out. The money, the offer, meant nothing to him. Yet meant all the wrong things to her. He knew she wouldn't accept because she was proud enough to want to go Dutch and couldn't afford it. So he was going to have to improvise. Fortunately, he knew where he could find some really good guidebooks.

And he'd show her New York.

'You want to get an idea of where things are,' he said as the car cruised along with the traffic. 'How the city works, in terms of design.' If she designed costumes, he figured she'd be interested in other aspects of design too. 'I have a plan for sustained sightseeing.'

'Oh, you do?'

'Uh-huh.' He nodded sagely. 'You don't want to cram too much into one day. You have the benefit of a whole month in New York—you can afford to take your time, get to some of the things that aren't on the usual lists, spend longer in some of the great places.'

'Okay.'

He grinned; he had her interest. 'So the rough daily plan is a gallery, a park, a place.'

'Daily plan?' she giggled. 'Like this is some sightseeing diet?'

'*Feast,*' he corrected in all seriousness. 'I'm assuming you're into galleries, right? Museums? Places to soak up inspiration?'

Her face lit up. 'Yes, please.'

'Then a park—some fresh air. A bit of a stretch, some greenery. And then a place.'

'A place?'

'Like a building, or another kind of attraction. Maybe something historical, whatever. Like Liberty. Sound good?'

'Sure. I'm happy to be in your hands,' she turned her head towards him and cooed.

Tease.

'All right, let's head to our gallery for today.' He had to

get out of the car before he hauled her across his lap and showed her what he really thought of the no-PDA idea. 'The Met. You okay with that?'

'Absolutely.'

Twenty minutes later they got out of the cab. James told the cabbie to come back in a couple of hours and then pulled the paper from his pocket. He'd printed the e-tickets while she was showering this morning. Her eyes narrowed as she looked at them and registered what they were.

'I don't like queues.' He shrugged.

'I'm not a charity case.'

'You can buy me lunch in return.'

She looked up at him, her eyes very blue and fully serious. 'I'll hold you to that.'

'I know you will.' He ached to pull her close and kiss her and tell her not to worry about the damn price of anything. But he wasn't going to do that to her. He respected her need for independence. For space.

They were things he needed himself.

They walked into the Great Hall of the museum. She inhaled a deep breath, she even seemed to grow taller. Yeah, this was definitely what she'd needed.

He glanced around the interior—taking in the vaulted ceilings—and felt his own spirit revitalise. Yeah, he needed it too. To keep busy—his *mind* busy.

He let her pick which collections to tackle, happy to follow in her wake—the requisite 'five paces behind' perfect for checking out the inherently seductive sway of her hips as she walked. She wore another floral dress that accentuated her waist and the lush curves of her breasts. Ah, he shouldn't be thinking of her breasts. It was going to be hours before he could bare them and set his mouth over her pretty pink—

He slammed the brakes on his thoughts and stared hard at a painting instead.

Focus, James.

But it was hard. *He* was hard. Why had he thought trailing around a gallery, unable to touch her, would be a good idea? He gave up on looking at the painted 2D beauties and concentrated on the live, warm, real woman right in front of him.

'You don't want to take photos? Buy postcards?' he asked as they wandered from hall to hall.

'No. I put things in here if I need to.' She pulled a small sketchbook from her bag.

'You draw?' He peered over her shoulder to see the pages.

'Enough to remember what I need to.' She snapped it shut.

But he'd got a glimpse—small, neat, pencilled pictures. 'What kinds of things?' He was intrigued.

'Patterns. Ideas. Scraps of memory. But mostly it's all up here.' She tapped her temple. 'Treasures.'

Yeah, she was smart. Intense. Enthusiastic.

His brain wandered off course again. Hell, he needed some fresh air.

'So are we going to Central Park?' she asked when they finally headed back to meet the cabbie.

'That would be too obvious.' He grinned.

'Oh.' Her brows arched.

'This is a park where you wouldn't expect to find one.'

'Where's that?'

He pointed a finger to the sky.

'This is really cool—the views are amazing.' She almost bounced in excitement a half-hour later as they walked along the disused railway line that had been developed into an elevated, slim park. She turned to him and blushed.

'You've seen all this.' She glanced at him. 'I'm sorry if this is boring.'

'Never boring. I love New York.' Hell, he'd forgotten just how much fun the city could be. When *had* he last had a holiday? He honestly couldn't remember. Not a real holiday anyway; he always combined travel with work. 'And I've not seen any of this with you before. Come on.' He nodded to a stand ahead. 'You can buy me lunch.'

She glanced at him. 'You want this for lunch?'

'I love those pretzels.'

'Real carbs man, aren't you?'

He nodded. 'I find I need the energy at the moment.'

Laughing, she went to the stand and bought two of the giant, doughy pretzels.

She handed him one with a flourish. 'I know you're doing this to soothe my penniless pride.'

'Careful,' he said softly. 'Looking at me like that might make me want to kiss you.'

'Uh-uh.' Laughing, she stepped a couple of paces ahead of him.

They walked along the High Line, eating. Ruefully he pondered how amazing it was that the decision not to touch made him so aware of how close she was. How easy it would be *to* touch. He glanced up and saw she'd caught him—no doubt his thoughts had been written all over his face given she was blushing now. But she shook her head provocatively, as if she were the mistress remonstrating with the misbehaving boy. She was going to pay for that. Later.

'We'd better keep moving,' he growled. 'The Public Library,' he instructed the cabbie when he met them at the end of the park.

'The lions are called Patience and Fortitude,' James informed her as they walked towards the entrance a short-ish drive later. 'Which do you identify with?'

'Definitely Fortitude,' she answered wryly. 'And you?'

'Patience,' he groaned. 'I need much patience today.'

'Poor James,' she cooed. 'Are you suffering?'

She had *no* idea.

The library was beautiful, stunning, fascinating. Just like her. James struggled to contain the rising sense of impatience as they slowly walked through the massive reading room. But he was determined to control himself—and his wayward urges. He could do something for someone else, put someone else's needs first...

Except he was starting to wonder what her needs might be right at this time. She was looking at him more than she was looking at the building and the treasures within.

'James?' she asked softly—all the sass gone. Her blue eyes had gone smoky.

'You got lunch, I've already got dinner.' He sent her a quelling look and marched her back to the waiting cab. 'No arguing. Central Park please,' he called to the cabbie. 'Best entrance for the Delacorte.' He couldn't let her derail his carefully laid plans. Not so quickly.

'Sure.'

James peeked into the basket the driver had collected for him while they were at the library. 'Thanks,' he said as the car pulled over. 'We'll see you tomorrow.'

'Nine-thirty?'

'Perfect.'

But when he followed Caitlin out of the cab, she stood in his way, her hands on hips. 'See him tomorrow?'

'He owes me big time.' James nodded, switching the basket to his other hand.

'James—'

'Shall we go to a show?' He walked past her towards the park, ignoring her half-frustrated laugh. 'Come on.'

'James!'

'Don't worry.' He pointed to a poster. 'It's free. All the tickets are free.'

Diverted, she stopped and scanned the print. Her gaze flickered to him accusingly. 'I don't recall you queuing for tickets today... How did you do this?'

'Pulled strings,' he answered honestly. 'And I have a picnic in here for us to have first.'

One thing he could do was organise.

'Thank you.' She stepped in front of him, looking up at him. 'I mean it. Thanks for taking me to all these places today. I have had the best time.'

So had he. But honestly? The best was yet to come.

'You just thanked me?' He opted to tease her—mainly to stop himself from pulling her close and plundering her mouth the way he'd been thinking of for hours now. 'Have I finally redeemed myself in your eyes?'

'Hmm.' She put a hand to her chin and pretended to think about it. 'Maybe one more night of sexual slavery will do it.'

James groaned, hard and hurting. 'Don't torment me. We have hours of Shakespeare to sit through first.'

He was almost bursting out of his skin with desire for her. Why had he agreed to the no-PDA idea? Madness.

She was aware of it too—sending him sly looks. Her cheeks and lips reddened, her eyes big and sparkling. She was a minx. He knew she was sitting just slightly too close, knew she was acutely clued into his physical discomfort. And she was maxing it out for the fun of it.

Yeah, she was trouble.

He tried to concentrate on the play, truly he did. But it got about forty per cent of his attention tops. Mostly he sat watching her, watching the play. He delighted in her delight. And he couldn't wait to have her home alone and all his.

If they stayed this busy, it'd be okay. The two weeks would go by fast enough and then he'd get back into the usual routine—work, work, work, sleep. But for now he tried to think up more plans: what else they could do for free—or for very little—in New York. Only he kept glancing at her, his awareness of her so acute it hurt.

Finally the play ended. They walked through the park to the condo. The air was warm enough but the atmosphere between them sparked as if an electrical storm were raging. They didn't speak. He was too ragged and near the edge to manage it and he could hear the little shallow breaths she was taking. Was she as keyed up as he?

It wasn't possible.

But as they rode the elevator up to his condo they faced each other—each with a back to the wall, keeping that distance between them by tacit agreement. Because the second he touched her he'd be out of control.

She knew—her eyes gleamed with that knowledge. She *was* the same. She was already on fire—because her hands clutched her dress. He hissed out a breath as she lifted the hem up her legs a couple of inches. She leaned right back against the wall, her legs parted. Her breasts rose and fell quickly as she lifted her dress higher still.

'I want you,' she said.

James swore, grabbing her wrist and striding out of the elevator the second the doors slid open. He unlocked the condo as quickly as he could, pulling her inside and slamming the door. He hauled her close and kissed her like the sex-starved animal he was. Furious satisfaction roared through him as she slid her arms around him and clung, opening instantly for him. Quickly, desperately, he worked to undo his trousers enough to release his agonised cock and sheath it, kissing her still, claiming the cavern of her mouth with his tongue.

He needed to claim all of her.

He pushed her back against the wall and dropped to his

knees. Thankful she wore a dress. Thankful she moaned and spread her legs and let him. Just thankful.

He skimmed his hands up her inner thighs, his haste fuelled by her breathlessness, her willingness, her revealing heat. Beneath her dress, he pulled aside her panties and kissed her intimately, tasting her readiness, loving the clenching of her sex as she came. He loved her quick response, loved that he had to secure her hips in a firm hold because she writhed so wildly. Dominant, victorious instincts flared. He shredded her knickers so he could delve deeper with his fingers and tongue. He loved to make her take more—give her more of that unbearable pleasure until she bent double, her hands tearing his hair as she screamed for mercy. And screamed in release. Then he just gave her all of him. Pulling her to the floor and driving home.

The expression on her face when he entered her… The unutterable pleasure of being inside her… He was possessed of the primal demand to thrust, ride, own. She was his woman—to pleasure, to hold, to enjoy. Vitality, victory flowed through him as he entered her realm. Their chemistry was nuclear powerful, their bodies brilliantly compatible. He'd never tire of the sexy sighs she released as he wound her higher again. He gritted his teeth, bucking like a wild animal, driving them both full speed to oblivion.

It was minutes before he could see again, could breathe easily again. With a rueful smile he rolled off her, kicking his legs free of his trousers. He scooped her into his arms, loving the way she clung—not just with her arms, but with her dazed eyes.

No wonder people got fixated on sex. Who'd have thought it could be so restorative? Was he really that shallow that all he needed was regular sex to keep him happy? But this was vastly different from the wild-oats, different-woman-a-week phase of not that long ago. Different in that this was with the same woman.

His gut tightened. No, it wasn't just sex. It was sex with Caitlin. And there was no one in the world like Caitlin. He carried her up to bed, running his hand down her smooth, pale skin, appreciating the way she arched into his touch as he placed her on the mattress. Undeniably pretty, yes, but also smart, spirited. Sassy.

And sad. It appeared in her eyes when she thought he wasn't looking. In the moments before he touched her and made her forget everything. Or before he teased her about something and made her laugh. He liked it when she laughed.

So he ran his fingers down the vee of her dress now, teasing as he unbuttoned it and got her blessedly naked. He pinned her down to kiss her and summon the sighs and smile he found so addictive. He loved that it was so easy.

Nothing felt as good as her climaxing around him, her cries filling his ears, her hot damp body collapsing as he wrung the last drops of tension from her. She was as eager for abandonment as he, passionately throwing herself into the heat that flared between them. Physical was everything. It wasn't always fast; sometimes he made it a slow drawn-out tease.

And it was always pure ecstasy.

CHAPTER EIGHT

THE SATED FEELING never stayed. James, himself, never stayed. Not anywhere. Not even in bed. And Caitlin had cottoned on quick.

'Do you never sit on a park bench? Never lie down in the grass?' she teased as they walked through the Riverside Park after they'd been to the Guggenheim.

'No. I like to keep busy.' He fobbed her off with a smile.

'You don't know how to relax?'

'I don't like being bored.' He didn't like lying still. If he wasn't kept busy, his brain started to replay things he preferred to forget.

'No rest for the wicked?' she joked.

'That's right,' he answered with a smile, but was perfectly serious.

So for the next few days they stuck with the plan—gallery, park, place and no PDA. They took in an outdoor screening of a classic movie at Bryant Park, rode the Staten Island Ferry past the Statue of Liberty, walked down Wall Street, went to several indie, abstract, out there galleries in Chelsea. They visited memorials and museums, watched musicians in parks, stood by sculptures, went to another Broadway play, lunched in Little Italy, Chinatown, and ate yet more from street vendors, from urban markets, scoffed pancakes in small diners. They explored the flag-

ship stores—from Apple to Lego to Tiffany's—and the bou-
tiques in the Meatpacking District, Tribeca. He kept them
on the schedule—and he was liking it a hell of a lot more
than he'd ever thought he would. They saw loads, talked
incessantly, laughed often.

But on the fourth day, Caitlin rebelled.

'My feet *hurt*,' she explained.

She marched to a stand and bought herself an ice cream.
'You want one?'

He shook his head. 'Come on.'

'No,' Caitlin said bluntly. She was not walking another
five miles around a park. It wasn't that she was unfit or anything, but she just wanted to sit. It was a beautiful, sunny
day. She wanted to watch the world go by and relax.

'No?'

'No.' Passive resistance. That was the way. She took
her ice cream and walked onto the spring lawn, selecting
a spot far enough away from other people for some privacy—though she still planned to enforce the no PDA rule.
It made life fun. 'You can sit for ten minutes.' She told him.
'It's not that hard.'

He rolled his eyes. 'Ten.'

'Maybe twenty—it's a big ice cream.' And she proceeded
to lick it ve-e-ery slowly.

He muttered something unintelligible under his breath
and flung himself down on the grass beside her. Caitlin
ignored him, just kept on licking her ice cream. He turned
his head to the side, she knew he was staring at her, willing her to look at him. She wasn't going to. Ten minutes of
doing nothing. How hard could it be?

She rested back on one hand, enjoying the warmth of the
sun, the taste of the ice and the fascinating mix of people
making the most of the park. So many people. So much to
see. And someone so gorgeous to do it all with…

She glanced down to flash him a quick teasing smile but to her utter astonishment his eyes were shut. Was he asleep? She leaned closer. His face was fully relaxed, his breathing regular, deep, slow. Oh, he was asleep. And gorgeous. Warmth flowed through her—not just the usual 'I-need-to-jump-him' warmth, but something else. She sat back, crumbled the last of her cone and tossed it for a pigeon or twenty.

Holiday fling, Caitlin. Just lust.

She could remember that, right? Because that was all this could be. But she looked down again, fascinated to see him like this. Almost vulnerable, utterly relaxed. And a little alone. She felt oddly protective of him. She'd known he'd been tired, but he never seemed to want to stop—why was that? Why couldn't he give himself a day or two to just laze about? He so obviously needed it. He might even enjoy it if he gave himself the chance.

A kid suddenly bellowed—a sound of despair and outrage. Caitlin glanced up and winced. The poor little girl had dropped her ice cream. Caitlin hoped the indignant wails wouldn't wake James. But of course they did. His eyes snapped open, that slight edge returned, that tension never seemed to leave him. It was a thread running right through his fabric. Caitlin smiled ruefully, wishing he hadn't woken and that he'd been able to relax a little longer.

'Hell, I fell asleep?' Looking sheepish, he sat up. 'You should have woken me.'

'Don't worry, you didn't snore.'

He didn't look any more comfortable, if anything he looked more embarrassed. And confused. 'I *never* sleep in public places.'

Coyly amused, she shrugged. 'Guess you must need it.'

'You think?' He drew in a deep breath and then released

it with a huge sigh. He looked at her and smiled, that winning, slightly wicked smile. 'I have to go to a gala tonight.'

She lifted her brows, not sure what he wanted her to say.

'Fundraiser, for the foundation I work for. There'll be benefactors there. Medical people. All kinds really.'

She was pondering a benign reply when he spoke again.

'Come with me.'

'No.'

'What if I said please?'

'No.'

'Why not?'

'Leaving the invite a little late, aren't you?' She cocked her head. 'If it's tonight.'

He smiled wryly. 'I wasn't sure you'd have something to wear and I didn't think you'd let me *Pretty Woman* you.'

'You were right, I wouldn't,' she admitted. But his frankness eased one of her reservations.

'Then I decided I didn't care what you were wearing,' he continued, 'so long as you're there with me. But I didn't want you to feel uncomfortable.'

'I won't,' she said quietly, her breath stolen by the sweetness of his comment. 'I have something to wear.' She always packed one glam dress, because you just never knew and because she'd spent hours making it and couldn't bring herself to leave it behind.

'So you'll come?'

She shook her head. It so wouldn't be wise.

'I need you there.' The wickedness entered his eyes. 'You'd be protection for me.'

'Protection?'

'From all the women who've read that article.' He waggled his brows.

'Oh, from the hordes throwing themselves at you, you

mean?' she said tartly. She so didn't want to witness that, thanks.

'That's right.' He winked, back to all arrogant. 'And you know it's too posh for paparazzi,' he said in a conspiratorial stage-whisper. 'The place will be full of the elite, discreet New Yorkers who have no desire to be pictured in any society magazine. There won't be any hounds there. They're not allowed.'

Admittedly she was tempted. But it was still too public. 'Wouldn't it contravene the terms of our contract if I went as your date?'

'You're a real stickler for that, huh?' He rose onto his knees and placed his palm over his heart. 'What if I, James Wolfe, do solemnly declare to touch you not?'

Hmm. Not bad. It helped that he was on his knees—it made her smile. 'No kissing. No dancing.'

'Not even dancing?' He looked aghast. 'Just scintillating conversation?'

'That's as good as it gets.'

'Then let's not bother with a "place" this afternoon.' He stood and started walking. 'You'll want to go home and get ready, right?'

She nodded.

Turned out James' idea of getting ready meant aerobic, intimate acts of pleasure lasting nigh on two hours, leaving her not nearly long enough to get ready. In the end she marched him to the shower—using any and all seductive means necessary—and then banished him from the room so she had the personal space to put on her make-up. Not that she needed blusher—her cheeks had the glow that only multiple orgasms could bring.

Forty minutes later he knocked on the door. 'Are you ready?'

As ready as she'd ever be for something so daunting. She

gulped in an extra hit of oxygen before opening the door. Then she went giddy.

'You scrub up pretty well.' She coughed. Understatement. *Vast* understatement. 'Total Cary Grant.'

The black tux fitted him in that way that only bespoke could. It was the most formally dressed she'd seen him and he looked devastatingly debonair.

'And that's some dress you're wearing.' He stepped into the room, shutting the door behind him, not taking his eyes from her.

'It's appropriate?' she asked, anxiously turning towards the mirror to ensure the layers of green silk were sitting properly.

'No.'

'What's wrong with it?' Wide-eyed, she spun back to face him.

He paused, watching the way the skirt flared as she moved. 'What's wrong,' he said slowly, 'is that I take one look and want to rip it from you. It clings—'

'It's tarty?' she all but shrieked in panic.

'No.' He laughed. 'No, no, no.' He reached out, lightly running his hands over her bare shoulders, pausing to toy with the delicate thin straps. 'It's not tarty or inappropriate. It's perfect. It hints at curves… It suggests…' He stepped closer.

'You can't do this,' she said, breathlessly stepping back out of his reach. 'You'll ruin my make-up.'

'But you look incredible.'

'That's very nice. I want to stay incredible.'

He drew a deep breath and then released it. 'Then we'd better go.'

They walked out of the building. Caitlin choked on a laugh as she saw their taxi driver waiting for them. 'You have this guy permanently on your payroll, don't you?'

James just winked.

His assurances were correct—there were no paparazzi. It was very dignified, discreet and yet opulent. You could almost smell the money in the air. The room sparkled with jewels, silk and satin. But the majority of the people present were over the age of forty.

'Where are your hordes?' she whispered as he passed her a champagne flute.

'Cougars,' he whispered back. 'The scariest of all.'

He walked over to a very small, elderly woman.

'Peggy, may I introduce you to Caitlin? She's a friend of the family visiting us from London for a while.'

Caitlin smiled at the woman, warmed inside by James' introduction of her. He'd made it clear she wasn't his 'date', knowing how much privacy mattered to her. She appreciated it. And this woman was no octogenarian cougar. They chatted pleasantries for a bit, talking about places Caitlin had visited, Peggy offering advice on where else she should visit. Caitlin relaxed, realising that for the first time she was just 'Caitlin'—not Hannah's sister, not Dominic's ex, not the wild child failed telly diva. She was just herself and this woman had no preconceptions. No judgment. It was liberating.

'I really do like your dress,' Peggy commented. 'I hope you don't mind my asking who the designer is?'

He'd only been half listening to the conversation, but James now tensed as he saw the colour running up under Caitlin's skin. Why? She looked incredible—the dress fitted her like a glove. Was it from some off the rack chain store and she was worried about admitting that?

'Actually I made it myself,' she answered, her chin lifting.

'You did?' he interrupted, startled.

Caitlin turned to him with a glint in her eye. 'Well, I did

study costume design, James. I ought to be able to make a dress.'

Well, yeah. He guessed so. But that wasn't just a dress; in his opinion that was a masterpiece. It fitted her so beautifully, just like— He paused. Realising. All her other dresses? She'd made those too? She was talented.

Peggy cackled at his obvious surprise and went back to her interrogation of Caitlin. 'You don't want to do fashion design?'

'No.' Caitlin turned back to her. 'My heart really is in theatre design. Costumes.'

'Have you been to the Met yet?'

'Not yet. But I've seen a couple of Broadway shows and the Shakespeare the other night, in the Park.'

Yeah, he'd known Peggy was a good person to introduce to Caitlin. The woman was a major benefactor of the arts and theatre scene as well as the foundation. She knew everything and everyone of importance to do with it.

James smiled, relaxing for the first time since they'd got there. He should have invited Caitlin sooner—as soon as she'd agreed to come with him he'd felt better about the event himself. Just knowing she was going to be here— even if they weren't going to be touching—put something at ease within him.

'Well you must get to the Met,' Peggy was saying in her inimitable, authoritative way. 'The opera costumes are works of art. You have to see the detail up close to believe it. If you'd like I could put in a call, get you in there— backstage?'

Caitlin's blush was fiery, her eyes alight with excitement. 'Really?'

'It would be a pleasure. You could spend the day. Are you in New York for long?'

'A month.'

'Then you can spend two days,' Peggy declared. 'Now tell me what you thought of that Shakespeare set.'

James took a step back as Caitlin and Peggy leaned in together, fully engaged in the conversation. He felt as if his tie had been tightened, his whole chest constricted. The reminder of Caitlin's length of stay grated.

He watched her holding court with two women now, talking costumes and sets and fashion. Getting info, displaying her knowledge. Talking about some of the things she'd seen already. With *him*. He felt like interrupting and pointing that irrelevant fact out.

Well, hell, was he feeling left out of the conversation like some petulant child?

Impossible. He never felt left out. Because, he realised, he never really felt *in*.

He spent months of his life living in cramped quarters but he'd always been able to maintain a sense of isolation. Some degree of privacy—even if it was just within the confines of his sleep roll and a mosquito net. To be sharing a bed, bathroom, and his body with Caitlin, there was no degree of separation. Right now his life was incredibly intertwined with hers. They were involved with everything together—their every waking and sleeping moments. He shook his head. He couldn't be fretting about losing that intensity, could he? It wasn't *real*—it was just a holiday fling after all. Yet the thought of her spending the day without him—seeing those treasures without him?

Lord, he was tragic. He needed to push back and find some distance for himself. Some perspective. One of James' medical colleagues walked by and James collared him in relief.

'How long are you in town?' the doctor asked.

'Couple weeks,' James answered. 'Getting restless actually. If you need a hand with any tight shifts…' The guy worked at the hospital that James occasionally locumed in when in between assignments.

'You're kidding. You're offering to come and work?'

James nodded. Work was good. Consistent. Easy in terms of its emotional demands—he knew how to manage those. It wore him out—but not in a bad way. It didn't leave him unsettled. How the hell could a holiday leave him this unsettled?

'You never want time off?'

He wasn't sure he did. He hadn't had time off in so long and these few days with Caitlin... He wasn't sure how he felt—whether it was too much already or not enough. So he fudged answering, talked work for a while, then got talking sport, then back to business again with Lisbet when she arrived. He reminded her, and himself, that he was ready to go back to work whenever she needed him to. And he was, right?

Ready.

In the meantime Caitlin and Peggy and who knew who else kept chatting. He kept half an eye on her but she was fully engaged. For ages. He was almost angry by the time Caitlin turned back to him as Peggy walked away to speak with someone else. She took one look at his face and her brows lifted.

'You spent hours talking to her,' he whispered in her ear as he handed her a fresh glass of champagne.

'What?' she answered back sassily. 'You missed me?'

Part of him sure had. And it wasn't the obvious. And there was the problem.

Caitlin kept stealing surreptitious glances at James as they chatted to various people for the next hour or so. He was very smooth, very polite, maintaining conversation on all kinds of topics. Yet she sensed his mind wasn't fully focused on the event at all. That inside, he was thinking about something else altogether. And for once she didn't think that something else was sex. Indeed, despite the impression she had that he didn't really want to be there, she didn't feel as if he was champing at the bit to leave either. She'd been thrilled at the possibility of getting in backstage at the theatre, but what she'd overheard now overshadowed that. Was he over them already? Was that why he'd offered to work at the hospital? Was he ready to fling their fling?

She smiled, she chatted. She tried not to care.

Back at the condo he sat down on the edge of the bed with a sigh.

'You're tired?' she asked blandly, still trying not to care.

He didn't answer. Just sent her a killer, heated look. His eyes black, his thoughts clearly back to carnal.

Oh. My. The coldness within Caitlin melted. Heat surged violently through her veins.

'No kissing? No dancing?' He growled. 'You almost killed me.'

'You want me to make it up to you?' She straddled his lap, her knees sinking into the mattress on either side of him. He put his hands firmly on her waist. She inhaled deeply as she felt his strong thighs shift beneath her. Definitely not tired.

The intensity of his expression didn't lessen. He looked fierce, almost angry.

'What are you thinking about?' She cupped his jaw, running the pad of her thumb over his lips.

His tongue chased her thumb and he groaned as he caught a small lick. 'That this holiday is unreal.'

Unreal? Was that good or bad? She chose not to ask, but to tease instead. They did tease so well. She pulled her hand free, dropping it to her hip. 'Yet you offered to do some shifts at the hospital.'

His breathing hitched. 'You heard that?'

'Why do you want to work?'

He shrugged but she'd felt his initial flinch.

'I might as well do something useful,' he said.

'You do something useful all the rest of the time. You're allowed a holiday.' She walked her fingers up his chest. 'You *need* a holiday. Otherwise you'll get burned out.'

'Are you concerned for my welfare?' He was smiling, but there was an underlying note of *something* in the softly asked question. A warning? An edge. As if he was wondering what business was it of hers?

Time to back-pedal. 'No,' she said. 'My concern is that if you start putting all your energy into work, what's going to be left for me?'

Her words pulled a low laugh from him and he leaned forward, sliding his hand on her back to draw her closer. 'You don't need to worry. I think I can still manage to turn you on.'

She pressed her palm to his chest, stopping him from bringing her close enough to kiss. 'You only "think"?'

'I promise to save enough energy to be able to satisfy you. That okay?'

'It'll do. Just.' She wanted more than satisfaction for herself. She wanted his as well.

His hand clamped over hers, holding it over his head.

'So it's okay for you to want to work, but not me?' he baited.

Was he bothered by the idea of her spending a couple days at the theatre? She tilted her chin high as she whispered, 'You're easier to get off than I am.'

He laughed roughly. 'You think?'

'Oh, yeah.' She nodded seriously. 'So easy.'

'That right?' he asked slowly.

She saw the dare in his eyes. 'You think you can hold out on me?'

'I don't just "think".'

'Such a man. Have to have the challenge, don't you?'

'That's right. We can't deny a dare.' He shifted beneath her. 'And you women know it. That's why you dare us with just a look.'

'Like this?' She inclined her head and coyly looked at him. 'So you're going to try to resist?'

'For as long as I can,' he confirmed, releasing her to stretch his arms out behind him on the mattress. He spread his feet a little further apart.

'You're already hard,' she pointed out with a quick stroke.

'Admittedly, this may be one dare I lose. But really, it's a win, win deal.'

'True.' She shrugged. She liked a dare too. She wanted to turn him on to the point where control was impossible. She wanted to do that *fast*. Yet there was pleasure in slow. Pleasure in stringing things out for him. Making him ache for more—unable to stop himself moving to reach for more.

She slipped off his knee and knelt on the rug. She looked up at him, unable to stop her smile. Usually he led their dance, liked the dominant role. The chance to take him, tease him, thrilled her. Because while it might look as if she were bent low to serve him, she was really setting out to conquer.

It didn't take long. His hands fisted in the coverings. She felt the tension, the effort it cost him not to lose control as she caressed him. And she revelled as she sucked him hard and heard his pained groan.

'Hell, Caitlin,' he gasped. 'What are you doing to me?'

CHAPTER NINE

JAMES LEAPT ON the phone to stop it screeching. Damn thing. He should have pulled the plug from the wall. 'Yeah?' he whispered, glancing at Caitlin's motionless form.

'You're still in town?'

James winced as he heard the reproach in his father's voice. Hell. Here he was having the time of his life in a no-holds-barred sexual marathon with a virtual stranger instead of going to see his family. How did he explain that? 'Ah...things got delayed.'

'Delayed for how long?'

'I'm not sure. I could be called away any day.'

Caitlin's head lifted, her blue eyes sardonically skewered him. He put a finger over her lips.

'Come home, James,' his father growled. 'You should see your mother.'

James swallowed. He hated the disappointment he heard. But he deserved to feel bad. 'I'll see what I can do.'

Caitlin didn't take her eyes off him the entire rest of the stilted phone call.

'I don't want to go,' he said belligerently the second he replaced the receiver on the cradle.

'Why not?'

'You know, I haven't asked you for the exact specifics

of what happened in London,' he snapped. 'We're allowed some privacy.'

Caitlin immediately withdrew, slipping out of the bed. 'I'm sorry,' she said quietly, making a dash for the bathroom. 'I guess I was concerned. I apologise for overstepping the boundaries.' But only a pace away the anger hit and she wheeled back to face him. 'But I'll just say this, James. I'd love to have a family who cared about me the way yours obviously cares about you,' she spat. 'Be grateful for what you have.'

He stared at her, a stunned look on his face—followed by anger, followed by...*what?*

She didn't know, but rigidly she stared him out. He looked so stunned—did no one pull him up on his bad behaviour?

He sighed and closed his eyes. A groaning growl emerged from somewhere deep in his gut. 'You're right.'

She was.

'I know you're right.' He kept his eyes shut. 'I'm sorry I snapped. I was feeling guilty. I'll go see them.'

Would that make him feel less guilty? About *what?* 'Great.'

He peeled one eye open and looked at her. 'You have to come with me.'

'What?'

The other eye snapped open and he sat up, the vital energy sizzling from him again. 'It's the only way I'll go. You promised me unlimited sex for the time I was back in the country.'

'Back in New York,' she clarified.

'This is still New York,' he said carelessly. 'The cottage is in the Hamptons. You don't come with me, I don't go.'

She stared at him as if he was loco. Which clearly he was. 'I can't just turn up to your family home uninvited.'

'I'm inviting you.' He flopped back onto the pillows.

No, that still wasn't okay. 'Your family will get the wrong idea.'

He looked amused at her concern. 'What—would it be so dreadful if they thought you were my girlfriend?'

She clamped her mouth shut for a second. Then breathed. 'It wouldn't be honest.'

'We're having sex round the clock. It's not entirely dishonest.'

'We're having sexual relations, not a relationship,' she said crisply, ignoring his laughter. 'And it's precisely because of that, that it's not a good idea if I come.'

'Your coming is a very good idea. There's nothing I like more.'

'Juvenile innuendo aside,' she said loftily, 'I don't believe this is sensible.'

'You didn't want sensible. You wanted fun. And I can promise you fun.'

She was diverted by that tone in his voice. The thread of promise. 'Wicked fun?'

'So wicked you might not be able to walk.'

She stared at him. The extent to which he turned her on with just a look and a laughing tease was appalling. She didn't want to have any nights without him. Not when she was having so few as it was. She didn't want to miss a minute. And besides all that, she was curious. She wanted to know more about him. Wanted to understand why it was he didn't want to go there without dragging a distraction with him.

He smiled. He knew he'd won. 'I'll tell them you're a friend of George's staying here—which is true—and that you're coming to see some more of the US of A. I'll even get you a separate bedroom. They won't suspect a thing. I'm very good at sneaking around the house.'

'I'll bet,' she said acidly.

He laughed. 'We'll go for a night. Maybe two.'

'How are we going to get there?' She frowned, all the practical problems hitting her at once.

He sat up and reached out for her wrist, drawing her back to sit on the bed beside him. 'Well, I was planning on taking a car. If you can't cope with coming in a car I've paid for, you could try to hitch a ride. Or you could go by train and we'll pretend we don't know each other at all...'

She elbowed his ribs. 'Smarty pants.'

'If you want to be with me, you're going to have to put up with my making the travel arrangements. I'm very good at travel arrangements. It's a family thing.'

'I still don't—'

'Look,' he growled and pulled her closer, his hands shaping her curves. 'I want you with me. That's the only way I'll go. If you want to see me make happy family time with my parents then you just have to suck it up. I'm not paying you for sex. You are under no obligation to do whatever with me even if I pay for your travel arrangements.'

She chuckled and clutched at his shoulders as he rolled above her. 'You really can't forgive yourself for that mistake, can you?'

Three—lazy tourist fun but PDA banned—days later Caitlin put on the seat belt in the front passenger seat of a sleek Porsche convertible. The drive wasn't nearly long enough for her to master her stupid nerves. And why on earth hadn't he visited them sooner when it was less than a couple of hours' drive?

'I thought you said this was a cottage?' Caitlin wheezed as they turned the corner and the house came into view. It wasn't like the kind of cottages they had back in England. This was a three-storeyed wooden mansion with separate accommodation wings, a car-turning bay, expansive lawns and formal gardens. And that was only what she could see from the roadside entrance. Heaven only knew what incredible features she'd find round the back—beach side.

'I shouldn't be with you.' She twisted towards him as he slowed down on the gravel drive. 'This is your family... your *mother*.' And a place that looked as if it would be featured in an episode of *Lifestyles of the Rich and Famous*. This was so out of her league.

'Don't worry about it. She doesn't bite. I, on the other hand, just might have to.'

'Stop it.' She elbowed his upper arm.

'Only if you stop worrying. As I said, I'm telling them you're George's special friend.'

But George was there, next to his parents, waiting at the top step to meet them. Along with another guy she didn't recognise. Both younger men lifted their eyebrows, then their eyes narrowed and swift, sly smiles appeared.

'Huh,' James grunted as he killed the engine. 'It's a whole damn family reunion.' He sent Caitlin an apologetic grin. 'We might have to improvise.'

Caitlin hung back but her awkward feeling was momentarily swamped by curiosity as she watched James walk quickly up to his mother and envelop her in a huge hug. In a second he'd turned back to her to introduce her to his parents and to his other brother, Jack.

Irene, James' mother, was petite, immaculately presented and had a beautiful, genuine smile.

'It's so nice of you to welcome me here. I know it was unexpected,' Caitlin said, wishing she weren't blushing.

Or that James was so obviously amused by her blush.

'It's a pleasure to have a friend of the boys,' said Irene.

Caitlin bit the inside of her cheek to stop herself laughing at the woman's reference to James, George and Jack as 'the boys'. They were giants next to her.

George winked at her. 'How're you finding New York?'

'Amazing. Thank you so much.' She smiled at him.

He nodded easily. 'When I left London Hannah had disappeared off the scene—buried in her manuscript research. I've never met a more "method" actress.'

Yeah, Hannah preferred to live her characters' lives. 'She gets very absorbed in her work,' Caitlin said, refusing to let anything other than pride and enthusiasm sound in her answer. She was aware of James' eyes on her as she answered. The disapproval she sensed from him about her lack of relationship with her sister was nothing short of ironic.

'Your sister's an actress?' Irene asked with a bright smile. 'You didn't want to act too?'

'I did do some acting work for a while,' Caitlin fudged. 'But I really don't have the talent or the drive. I'm happier backstage.'

'Oh? What do you do?'

Caitlin fixed a smile to her face and answered the kindly meant questions, all the while thinking of the dynamics. The polite welcome mat was fully unrolled for her, but there was no hiding the absolute joy in Irene's eyes as she'd watched James walk up to her. No hiding the way she'd hugged him as if it had been forever since she'd been able to.

Just how long had it been? And why? Was it really only work that kept James from coming home more often?

'I didn't know you were still here,' James said quietly to his twin as he watched Caitlin walk into the house with his mother. Jack had already gone ahead with his father, talking business no doubt.

'I didn't know you were bringing Caitlin,' George replied.

'She seemed lonely,' James said blandly. 'I thought she might enjoy a change of scene.'

'Nice to see you being social.' George's brows knitted together. 'How are the two of you rubbing along in the condo if most of the rooms are out of action?'

'We figured it out.' At George's sly smile, James rolled his eyes. 'You know how capable we are of bunking down when necessary.'

'When necessary.'

There was no fooling his twin. Not in many things.

'You haven't been here in a while,' George added.

'Mmm,' James mumbled a non-answer. 'How're you getting on in London?'

'Nearly done. I'll be glad to get home.'

'You're not enjoying that party lifestyle you appear to be living?'

George chuckled. 'I'm jaded, brother. All the pretty women blur together after a while.' He sent him a glance. 'Whereas I assume you're still doing the celibate monk thing?'

'Hard to find playmates the places I go to.'

'But you're in New York for a few nights now, right? Easy pickings.' George's gaze wandered to Caitlin again. 'Hard when you've got a roommate cramping your style though I guess.'

'Guess so.'

'But then she's a very pretty roommate.'

James wasn't biting. He *refused* to bite.

'I've always thought she was the prettier of the two,' George added.

'You of all people should know it's not nice to compare. Especially siblings.'

George laughed. 'Good deflection, but don't think I don't have eyes.'

James tensed. 'Look all you want.'

'But don't touch?'

James turned to face his brother head on. George wasn't the right guy for Caitlin. Then again, nor was James. 'Don't,' he said softly. 'Don't say anything, don't do anything...just leave her.' *Leave her to me.*

George mock-punched his shoulder. 'I'm your brother. Sometimes it seems like you forget that.'

James looked into the eyes almost as dark as his own. 'I never forget.'

'Then don't be such a stranger.'

Caitlin luxuriated in the shower, washing off the travel in the massive en suite. In fact the whole house was massive. The beachfront mansion had a small movie theatre, a bar, a spa and pool that overlooked their own private stretch of beach. It was unbelievably beautiful. But it wasn't all perfect show home. It was warm, with pictures of the family all around, and as she'd been given the tour by his mother Caitlin couldn't help but wonder why on earth James didn't want to be here.

She'd requested some time to take a shower before dinner, deliberately giving James some space to have time alone with his family. At the knock on her door, she wondered if she'd taken too long. But it was him—telling her that dinner would be in another half-hour.

'What have you been doing?' She stared at him. He was covered with a sheen of sweat and had that edgy gleam in his eye.

'Playing tennis,' he answered briefly, pacing away from her already. 'Half an hour 'til dinner, okay?'

She watched him walk down the hall, all popping muscles and curled-up fingers. What was with the hard-out tennis tournament within ten minutes of arriving? Wasn't this a place to relax and catch up with his family? But he seemed to be as restless as he'd been in those first couple of days in New York—until he'd calmed down a touch and managed to actually sit still for a few minutes at a time. Then again, maybe that was how he and his brothers bonded? With their own mini-Olympics.

But if that was the case, why did he still look bothered?

'We eat outside in summer, Caitlin.' James' mum smiled at her when she arrived in the lounge. 'You don't mind?'

James knew Caitlin wasn't going to mind. The wooden deck overlooked the pool and the beach—an unlimited view to the horizon. And Caitlin did like a nice view.

At dinner James focused on his food, but his appetite had taken a hike hours ago—the second he'd pulled into the driveway. He regretted coming here already. He felt Caitlin glance at him, knew she noticed his silence. But he wasn't the only quiet one: Jack was abnormally preoccupied tonight. James had seen him sneaking way too many looks at his mobile phone even for a workaholic like Jack. Something was on—the business, most likely.

'This is your first time to New York?' James' dad asked Caitlin.

James glanced at her as she admitted it was.

'What's been your favourite thing so far?'

'Oh, now that's impossible, I've seen so many amazing things,' she answered diplomatically. 'James has been an amazing tour guide.'

'James has?' his mum asked.

Inwardly he winced as he saw the stunned expressions in his parents' eyes. Even Jack looked up from his phone and sent him a sideways glance.

'Um…yeah.' Caitlin picked up on the prickle in the atmosphere and sent him a beseeching look. An apology? Uh huh. Too late she'd remembered he hadn't wanted to come home. That he'd told his family he was busy. She didn't yet know why he was so reluctant to be here, yet she was still sorry she'd dropped him in it.

He forced a grin, wanting to let her know it didn't matter. He didn't want her to feel awkward. 'I couldn't leave her alone to face the streets of New York,' he explained with a lazy shrug. 'Had to lead her through it. Wolves make the best guides, right?'

'That they do.' George chuckled.

'How nice.'

With a sinking heart James saw the interest and amazement in his mother's widened eyes. Oh, hell—what was she thinking now? That he was about to settle?

Never gonna happen, Mum. Sorry.

Damn. He listened as his mother pumped Caitlin for details on where he'd taken her in Manhattan. He knew he shouldn't have come back for this visit. And he should never have brought Caitlin. He was only ever going to disappoint them.

All of them.

He glanced over the table, willing the meal to be over so he could escape. Part of him just wanted to haul Caitlin off to his room. He ached to be near to her again. Touch her. Hear her laughter. It made him feel good when he made her laugh.

But it wasn't fair of him to use her as his distraction. It wasn't fair of him to avoid talking about anything other than work or safe travel topics with his family.

He knew he needed to try harder, but all he really wanted to do was run. He didn't know that he was ever going to be able to stare down the ghosts and memories that haunted him here, when he was with his family. When he was at work, it was easy. He loved to work.

Caitlin smiled her way through the amazing food and

wine in the relaxed, stunning setting. His parents kept conversation flowing and were polite enough to explain and include her in on the little family jokes that peppered the conversation. The topic turned to adventures further abroad. She figured it was inevitable given they published travel guides. Jack was the current head of the family company—and a serious globetrotter. George, a venture capitalist, travelled widely looking at different projects to pump his money into. And then James travelled a different kind of route—to disaster-hit cities and remote villages. Two out of the three brothers, and their parents, entertained her by regaling her with their worst travel exploits.

She was conscious of James' silence, of him watching her too closely. His gaze wandered a little too far south of her face every so often. He really shouldn't send her those smouldering looks when she was talking to his parents. She glared pointedly back at him but only got a wicked smile in return.

And she couldn't help feeling that they were all playing it 'safe' somehow. Especially James. She had the feeling she was his shield. That her presence kept the conversation perfectly light. More than ever she wondered what the leashed undercurrent within him was all about.

'I can't wait to get you alone,' he muttered as she helped him carry dishes inside after the meal. 'You owe me, you know.'

Yeah but she had to be polite first. And so did he.

Back on the deck, as the setting sun splashed the sky in red and gold, she studied him and his brothers. Jack was wholly different from the twins—not quite as tall, but more solidly built and with blue eyes that pierced in a slightly unnerving way. She wasn't sorry he was apparently welded to his mobile phone. Now she knew James so well she saw the scar was nothing on the real differences between him and

George. James' lips curved as he saw her looking from him to George and back again. His eyebrow flickered.

'Did you use to trick people when you were younger?' she asked.

'The people closest to us always knew. But we liked to try it on with new teachers.'

'Girls?'

'Never. We've always had different tastes when it comes to women. Well,' he corrected as George wandered closer, 'George just has gluttonous tastes, while I'm more discerning.'

George lifted his shoulders negligently. 'I see no reason to put limitations on myself. I love to love women. Lots of women.'

Caitlin chuckled.

'Don't encourage him,' James said drily. 'He'll only start to flirt.'

'What do you mean start?' George asked. 'I've been working on it all evening.'

'Flirt away,' Caitlin laughed. 'You'll get nowhere.'

'You've not decided to become a nun?' George asked, appalled.

'Hard as this may be to believe, I'm simply not interested.'

George blinked. 'Impossible.'

'Give it up, brother,' James roasted him. 'You have to face the fact that your usual technique has failed.'

'What's his usual technique?' Caitlin asked.

'Superficial.' James smiled, basically baring his teeth.

'Cruel, James,' George jibed.

'But accurate.'

'Come out with me, Caitlin,' Jack interrupted. 'There's no contest as to who's the most fun…'

'You guys have always been this competitive?' Caitlin asked.

'Ignore them, Caitlin,' Irene said calmly. 'They're fools. And no, Jack, you're not going out. This is the first night you've both been home in ages. You're to stay right where I can see you.'

'All right.' George winked at his mother, then turned back to eye Caitlin. 'I'll have to prove my superiority with the Scrabble board.'

'Scrabble?' Caitlin choked. Wow, they really were into the happy family scene here.

'Hell no,' James groaned. 'Not Scrabble.'

'You don't think you can handle it?' George teased.

'I'm actually quite good at Scrabble,' Caitlin said smugly. 'I'm pretty tough to beat.'

'*You're* up for Scrabble?' James stared at her.

'Absolutely.' She could see what he wanted but she was not diving away for an early night. It would be obvious to everyone what was going on.

She caught the glint in his eye as he replied, 'All right then, Scrabble it is. Jack, you in?'

'No.' Jack shook his head. 'I'm in the pool.'

Caitlin glanced at Jack for a moment as he cast off his shirt, dived into the pool in his boardshorts and proceeded to swim length after length. Yeah, they were a bunch of competitive sports types. Well, she couldn't compete with either the tennis or the swimming, but with Scrabble? She had half a chance. She pulled her chair closer to the table as James and George set out the board and pieces.

She'd endured hours of Scrabble as a young teen, it had been the on-set tutor's way of trying to beat the boredom of waiting for scenes. Caitlin hadn't exactly loved it, but now she took the game on fiercely. She planned on beating these boys. And twenty minutes later she was doing exactly that—*just*. She and James had leapt ahead of George who, it was fair to say, didn't seem to have his heart in it.

'There was me thinking you were all about sequins.' James frowned as she put down an eighty-seven point word by using a triple points square.

'I'm all about designing patterns,' she said primly. 'Oh, look at that,' Caitlin murmured, putting down another set of winning point letters.

George threw his hands in the air. 'I retire. You're too good for me. Couple of geeks,' he muttered under his breath.

James laughed. 'Jealous brother. You never could cope with me winning.'

'You haven't won yet,' Caitlin pointed out calmly, putting her last piece, an 'a', above another 'a' already on the board.

He stared at it. 'There's no such word as "aa". Acronyms aren't allowed in our version of the game.' He grinned gleefully.

'Actually "aa" is a form of solidified lava,' she said. 'Feel free to look it up if you need to, but I think you'll find I'm right. And that I've just won by a point.'

'Solidified lava, huh?' he asked.

'Yes.'

'That's right.' She tilted her chin. 'If you're up for it, you can always challenge me to a rematch.'

James' eyes narrowed. 'All right. But it has to be speed Scrabble.'

Thirty minutes later she chuckled. 'Did you want to try for best of three?'

'No, thanks. I concede the Scrabble crown to you.'

'And now, if you'll excuse me, I think I might retire.' Caitlin smiled, somewhat embarrassed.

She looked over at James' parents happily relaxing with all their sons home. Even if one of their sons hadn't been remotely relaxed.

She really shouldn't be intruding on this. Yet they'd made her welcome. She'd just been Caitlin again—with no cloud of doom hanging about her. Fitting in had been fun.

'Thanks so much for having me to stay,' she said. And meant it.

Ten minutes later there was a knock on her door and he slipped straight inside.

'What was with the delay?' he growled, pulling her close and spinning her to push her against the door. 'We could be on our third round by now.'

'I needed to flash my Scrabble skills.'

'Flash me some other things,' he muttered, his hands sliding over her dress. 'Fast.'

She laughed. 'But I won.'

'And I'm your prize.' He bent his head. 'I need to be in you. Now.'

His impatience was an incredible turn on. But there was something more that drew her to please him—that hint of raw.

'I never knew Scrabble could be foreplay,' she mused, teasing him as she began to unbutton his shirt.

'I've been waiting so long.' He looked into her eyes. 'I need this.'

Why? When they'd just had a perfectly pleasant night. But he kissed her before she could ask.

Sex. She reminded herself as she leaned into his kiss. It was just sex for him. It wasn't her he'd been waiting for. But the ecstasy, the physical release.

'You've been laughing all night,' he said, pressing kisses across her jaw line. 'Your laugh turns me on. I want to capture it. Capture you.'

'You have me,' she breathed, confessing the truth in a tease. 'Any way you want me.'

'Every way.'

Passion filled her. She needed to kiss him, touch him everywhere. Feel him. The thrill of being near him had never lessened. Chemistry was an incredible thing. She laughed now with the delight of it. Quickly he cupped his palm over her mouth. *Hard.*

Oh. Wicked excitement flamed inside her.

He smiled at her widened eyes. 'Can't have your sexy screams keeping everyone awake,' he whispered.

She twisted her head, lifting her mouth free of his muzzle. 'I don't scream.'

'Yeah, you do,' he taunted with a wicked smile. 'But first you sigh, then you pant. The panting gets quicker and louder. Then you scream.'

'I'm that predictable?' she asked, already breathless.

'Pretty much.'

'Keep your hands off my mouth,' she ordered in defiance. 'Your lips off mine. I can be quiet.'

'Can you now?' he dared.

Oh, hell, she wanted him so badly. 'You won't hear a peep. Promise.'

'But what if I were to do this to you?'

She jumped. Just slamming her lips together in time to stifle the yelp as he cupped her sex with an invasive hand, his thumb working in circles around her already swollen, pulsing clitoris.

His smile widened and he stepped in closer, bracing his other hand on the wall beside her head. 'You're really going to stay silent?'

Slowly she nodded, knowing they were in a game now. The thing about James was that he liked a challenge. Well, so did she.

'You think you're so tough,' he said softly. 'A tough nut to crack.' His mouth curved again and he leaned close to nip her lips. 'Like a macadamia. Delicious. But so hard to break into.'

'I'm not a nut,' she whispered furiously.

He chuckled loudly.

'If you don't want people to hear us, then *you* need to whisper,' she hissed.

Suddenly he moved, bending to pick her up. In three strides he deposited her on the bed. Coming down hard on top of her. She gritted her teeth to hold back her groan of delight. She loved taking his weight.

But then he lifted away and started to torment her. His hands feathered over her skin in horrendously slow, delicious strokes. He carefully lifted her dress, exposing her to him inch by inch. Touching, tasting every part of her as he revealed it. He slipped the dress from her shoulders. Pressed kisses along the edge of her bra as he worked to unclasp it. Then he went to work on removing her knickers.

Slowly, teasing. Sending her insane.

She reached for the pillow, bit down on the corner of it, clenching down on the torture. So close to coming. But she couldn't squeal.

'That's cheating,' he reproved, pulling the pillow out from her teeth.

Her jaw snapped. She breathed hard. 'Bastard.'

'Insulting my mother when you're in her home?' he chuckled. 'Bad girl.'

'And you're the bad boy for sneaking around to have sex with one of the guests on the sly?'

'You were the one who wanted this to be clandestine.' He gazed down her body as he slid his fingers along her slick sex. 'So let's have a silent orgasm then.'

He bent and added his mouth, his tongue to where his fingers already played. His mouth was hot and wet and wicked. His tongue skilled, his fingers fast.

Her lips parted, her head thrust back. He licked her again and again. He reached one hand up to her breast, strumming her nipple. The other hand working between her legs moved faster. One finger, two, three. He filled her while sucking and licking and kissing. Until she was rocking her hips like an animal, wildly running her hands through his hair.

She drew a deep, burning breath. Held it. Releasing it harshly as the sensations tumbled through her. Roughened breathing was not screaming. She'd done it.

'Not bad,' he said matter of factly, as if he were judging a cake contest. 'But I like it most when you've completely lost control.'

He stood from the bed, roughly removing his clothes as quickly as possible, rolling on a condom he'd pulled from his trouser pocket. And then he pinned her.

His hands gripped hers, pushing them to the mattress, his full weight on her body. His legs pushed hers wider apart as he plunged to the hilt.

She clamped her mouth shut, barely able to hold back the moan. He kissed down her neck, across the vulnerable skin over her throat.

'I can feel the vibrations of your silent sighs,' he teased.

He shifted position so his pelvic bone ground harder against hers, creating intense friction. Sensations hammered her as he made use of her. She was his to do with as he wished. Whatever he wished so long as it was like this. He was so strong, his sensuality so powerful. Her head thrashed side to side as she tried to hold back. But he escalated his onslaught, surging forward, thrusting fierce and fast.

'You like it when I'm inside you,' he commented hoarsely.

She'd never felt anything so good in her life.

'James,' she panted desperately. 'I'm going to scream.'

He slammed his mouth over hers, muffling the high,

keening noise as she came. And in return, she thirstily swallowed his uncontrolled, animal growls.

James was late to breakfast. He'd peeled himself away from Caitlin's side early in the morning and gone for a long run. Now they were all there at the table—Caitlin as well, looking like butter wouldn't melt. He couldn't help but give her a quick grin. But then he glanced at the food laid out on the table. His post-run warmth chilled instantly. He picked up one of the small, golden breads and glanced at the other pastries. He knew them so well. Could even taste them already.

'These are Aimee's?' he forced himself to ask, hoping his voice didn't sound as husky to everyone else as it did to him.

The conversation stopped. Even Jack tore his gaze from his phone.

'Yes,' his mother answered quietly.

'How is she?' James carefully put down the brioche.

'She's well. The bakery is doing brilliantly. Your father picked these up from there first thing. She's away at the moment though—Malibu.'

So he wouldn't have to see her—face her this trip. But that didn't change anything. And he didn't want this conversation. He didn't take a seat. 'I just need to go and—'

He didn't bother trying to think of a reason. He was out of the room already. He'd be able to breathe again in a bit.

Caitlin sat at the table, unsure of what to do or say.

'I knew that was a bad way to go about it.' James' mother sighed and left the room through another door—his father following closely.

Caitlin chewed on her one bit of brioche for a really long time. Go about what? Who was Aimee? Why had the mention of her name sent James into such an obvious lockdown—and spiked the tension in the family? Jack was back staring at his phone, only George was apparently still in 'good host' role—giving her a quick smile and offering her the plate of pastries and starting up a conversation on a completely unrelated topic. He was so damn determinedly cheerful and polite and easy-going that Caitlin knew it was all defence. She'd get nothing out of George. He was loyal.

'I'm going for a run.' George finally wrapped up his chat effort five minutes later. 'Why don't you check out the pool?'

'That sounds a great idea. Thanks.' She smiled at him gratefully.

She walked out onto the deck, thinking she'd check the pool temperature before committing herself. She paused. James was in there, furiously pulling through length after length after length as if he had Jaws on his tail. She walked over to dip in a toe, then bent to sit on the edge, letting her feet dangle in the cool water.

She knew he'd seen her. But he did another three lengths before coming over. Caitlin reached into her pocket and pulled out the small block she had in there. 'You want some?' She waved it in front of him.

'*My* chocolate?' He wiped the streaming water from his face. 'Give.'

Caitlin shook her head and tried not to ogle his gleaming body. 'Mine. I always keep some on me. It's a great travel tip I learned from this guy once.'

He grinned appreciatively and opened his mouth for her to put the piece in, keeping his wet hands away.

'You haven't had breakfast,' she said. 'And you've almost done like a triathlon or something this morning.'

He said nothing, just opened his mouth for another piece. She fed an extra large chunk to him.

'You can't relax here?' she asked. How the hell could he not relax?

'I like to stay fit.' He chomped and swallowed.

That wasn't all it was and she *wasn't* afraid to ask. Much. 'So who's Aimee?' She tried to ask as nonchalantly as possible. 'An ex-girlfriend or something?'

'What?' He looked utterly startled. 'No.' He shook his head, a slight grin appearing for an even slighter second. 'She was our housekeeper for years.'

'Oh.' Caitlin frowned. She was so missing something huge. Why would James get so awkward at the mention of their old housekeeper?

He stood waist deep in the water, watching her. A low, reluctant chuckle left his lips. 'I can see you clamping down on all those questions.'

She shrugged, making light of it. 'You don't want to talk? I'm not going to make you.'

He reached out and took the last of the chocolate from her fingers. He devoured the last bit in a gulp; she could see the small sustenance having an effect already. His smile was almost back. 'Thanks,' he said.

Thanks for the chocolate, or for not pushing him? She guessed both.

Of course now her curiosity burned brighter still.

James spent most of the morning deflecting conversation by engaging both Jack and George in another tennis round. Caitlin hadn't asked more about Aimee or what the connection was with him and his family, but it felt as if she'd withdrawn. She hardly looked at him. Logically he knew it was because she was too busy smiling and charming his family, not because she was bothered about him shutting her out. But even so, prickles pushed under his skin.

He whacked the ball hard and aced Jack. Was he shutting her out? He knew he was shutting his family out. He always had over this. There was nothing anyone could say to make it better or ease his guilt. Not even Aimee could say anything. And she'd tried to in the past—told him it wasn't his fault. That accidents happened. That people made their own choices. None of that made him feel any better. But he damn well refused to dwell and mope and stew. He stayed busy for very good reasons.

He didn't have to tell Caitlin. Didn't have to tell anyone. He'd acknowledged his actions, accepted the ramifications. The responsibility. And he'd moved forward with his life—on a far better course than he'd been before. He couldn't change the past, couldn't forget it, but it was better to make a difference and move forward.

But ironically, Caitlin *not* asking made him want to tell her. He wanted her to understand. He knew that she, of all people, wouldn't tell, certainly wouldn't judge. His lips twisted. Because she already knew he wasn't perfect, right? From the moment she'd met him, she'd had his number.

He was a fake.

CHAPTER TEN

'Come walk along the beach with me,' James said to Caitlin. It wasn't really an invitation, more a command. Because suddenly, it seemed vital that she did know it all. Why he'd suddenly morphed into a hyperactive sports freak. Why he couldn't sit still. Why he struggled to say anything particularly personal to his parents. Why he needed his life to stay the way it was.

She didn't hesitate. Didn't even answer. She just stood and followed him.

'Aimee was our housekeeper. She was married to Pete, our odd-jobs man,' he said roughly, as soon as they were out of earshot of the house. He didn't look at her as he spoke, but he felt her eyes on him.

'They lived with you?' she asked.

'They had a cottage at the other boundary. Kind of like the gate house, yeah.' He shrugged his shoulder, wincing at the obvious wealth. 'Louis was their only child. He was a couple years younger than us, smaller for his age. But we hung out all the time.'

They'd played together. Sometimes he and George had ganged up and played tricks. Other times the team would change and it'd be him and Louis against George and Jack. Looking back now he knew Louis had hero worshipped him a bit. Had been closer to him than the others.

'We were spoilt. We had everything. We were expected to be able to do everything. But sometimes kids don't make sensible decisions.' He let the waves wash over his feet. 'I thought I was invincible.'

She walked near him, her feet splashing softly. But she said nothing.

'We'd gone on a holiday to the Caribbean. A real "holiday" as opposed to serious "travelling". I was sixteen, living the life with all the toys. Yachts, jet skis...' It had been a playground for the rich and powerful and he'd been such an idiot. 'I told Louis I could handle it. I made him come out with me. Even though he didn't really want to. But I was filled with it—showing off. All arrogance.' He bent his head. 'I lost control of the jet ski, we flipped. Pete came out to help us. But he drowned saving the both of us.' James would never forget that horror as long as he lived. 'Louis lost his father and it was my fault.'

'What happened to Louis?'

'He'd lost his father.' James looked down. 'And he lost his way. Over the next few years it got worse and worse. He went off the rails, right into a fast, dangerous lifestyle.' The bright-eyed kid with the wide smile had become a pale, pimpled wreck of a youth with vapid eyes and the shakes. James' parents had tried. They'd all tried. But no amount of intervention was able to stop that downward spiral. 'In the end he died of an overdose.'

'Oh, James.'

'They said it was accidental.' He pressed his lips together.

James' guilt had grown. He'd gone the opposite way to Louis—pouring himself into his studies. Being perfect. Keeping himself so buried in textbooks and training there was no room for any other mistakes of that kind. He sobered up. Straightened out. Taking nothing for granted again. He'd made little time for fun. Yes he'd done the travel thing—the component required of all Wolves—but he'd done it tougher and with purpose. He'd chosen to study abroad and in his study, his work, he'd found salvation.

But at the end of the day, he'd been the cause of not one, but two people's deaths. Responsible for the devastation of a family. 'Pete had been a hero. He'd rescued us. I have to make something more of my life. He gave his life up for us. And then seeing Louis fall like that?'

'Louis might have gone off the rails even if the accident hadn't happened,' Caitlin said quietly. 'Even if his father had been around, it still might have happened. It happens in other families.'

James frowned. 'No. You should have seen how it hurt him.' He bent his head. 'I owe them. And I owe it to myself to make something more of my life.'

'That's fair enough. I can understand that.' She stopped walking. 'But not at the cost of your own happiness.'

'I'm not unhappy,' he denied, looking sharply at her. 'I love my work.'

'I know,' she said. 'But you've cut yourself off from your family.'

'I haven't.' Only a very little.

'No?' She grasped his arm when he went to turn away. 'You have limited interaction with them. With *all* relationships. You only have a woman when you can get it on a "firm boundaries" basis. And then you work. You put yourself at risk for others—for strangers—all of the rest of the time.'

'I *like* being busy.' He looked into her eyes. 'I know I made mistakes in the past. I can't ever change what happened. But I accept what I did and I've moved on.' He sighed. 'The only problem now is that my mother cries when I leave. I think it's easier on her not to visit.'

Caitlin vehemently shook her head. 'She's your *mother*. That's the way it's going to be. Maybe it wouldn't be so bad if she saw you *more* often. You can't stop your family loving you. Any more than you can stop loving them.' She stared up at him. 'Don't deny them the pleasure of having your company. Don't deny yourself. You still deserve to have a nice time, James. It's okay to take a holiday.'

'You care about me having a nice time?' he asked quietly.

Her alarm bells rang at the searching quality in his eyes. Because she *did* care—too much to be able to admit to herself, let alone to him. So she stepped back, hiding in the tease talk. 'Yeah, well, I find you perform better in bed when you're in a good mood.'

He burst out laughing. 'Shoot me down, why don't you, right when I've poured out my soul.'

It was because he *had* poured out his soul that she'd joked again. Because she knew he didn't like feeling vulnerable. And nor did she. Because she knew this thing between them couldn't go any further than it had already. 'I aim to please.'

'Actually—' he traced a finger down her jaw '—I think you do.' He added, 'I don't think you're all that bad at all.'

'Just misunderstood?' she drawled softly, trying to keep up the carelessness of her banter.

'Yes,' he answered, quite seriously. 'Misunderstood. Lonely. Lovely.'

She shook her head, tried to turn the conversation back on him. 'How come this never came up in any of those articles about you?'

'It was kept quiet.' His lips twisted and he cupped her face with a gentle hand. 'Ironic, isn't it, that you're accused of all kinds of things in the press that aren't true, while the truth about what an idiot I was has never been reported. It doesn't seem fair.'

'Life isn't fair.' Caitlin tilted her chin free of his hold. 'We all know that.'

She turned and walked back along the edge of the water. 'So where's Aimee now?'

'She set up her own bakery. She's an amazing cook.'

'And it's doing well?'

He nodded.

'Good for her,' Caitlin said softly.

'Yeah.'

Three hours later Caitlin was still mulling over what he'd told her. They'd spent the afternoon in a mini badminton tournament. She'd never played badminton before and had no idea she was so crap at it. But all the Wolfe boys were brilliant—and gallantly took turns teaming up with her, all still determined to beat their brothers despite having her handicap them. They'd made her laugh. Made her feel welcome.

Made her feel liked.

George flirted with her incessantly, Jack more intermittently. But it was the look in James' eyes that brought the colour to her cheeks. It wasn't lust.

She didn't know what it was.

'Come on, Caitlin.' George stood after the dinner plates had been cleared. 'Jack, James and I will show you some local nightlife.'

'We will?' Jack glanced up.

Irene laughed. 'Go on, then.'

'Um.' Caitlin avoided looking at James. She was sure he wouldn't want to. She sensed the restless energy in him. 'I really don't—'

'Yes, you do. Let's go.' James turned a brilliant smile on her.

Now she really wasn't sure this was a good idea. Because

that smile had an edge. For all the intimacy they'd had ear-lier—the part of his history he'd shared—he seemed in a more mercurial mood than ever. More edgy and unsatisfied.

The second they got to the lively bar James left his broth-ers to order drinks and gripped Caitlin's hand, leading her to the middle of the dance floor and pulling her indecently close.

'What happened to no PDA?' Caitlin gasped, breathless at the predatory expression in his eye.

'Hmm?' James answered vaguely, too busy staring at her cleavage.

She tugged at the top of her dress. 'Stop it. Your thoughts are written all over your face.'

'They are?' He looked up, his eyes almost black. 'Read them.'

He still thought he could win a dare with her?

She thought of the most explicit, crudest thing she could. Then found the courage to whisper it aloud in his ear.

His jaw dropped. Then he laughed. 'Damn, you're a vixen.'

She lifted her brows. 'You can be as naughty as you like with me. As bad as you get.'

His eyes glinted. 'That's what you really want?'

'It always has been.'

He tugged a swathe of her hair, so she tilted her head back. His words brushed over her lips. 'You act all sexy, demanding siren. But the thing is…' he leaned close '…that I know you'd let me do that and more. You might have been provoking, but there's a part of you that wants exactly that. You like it when I can't control myself.'

Well, that was true.

'A tease must be prepared to take the same,' he warned. He'd broken her control time and time again already.

And he knew it. But now he kept a firm grasp on her hair and kissed her.

'I thought we were keeping this under wraps,' she squeaked when he lifted his head. Hell, no one would be left in any doubt as to how well they knew each other if they'd seen that kiss.

'That was until you thought you could say something like that to me out in public. You thought wrong.' He slid his open palm all the way up her stomach, lifting higher to pluck her taut nipple.

'What are you doing?' She gasped.

'Turning you on.'

He already knew she was on.

'Here? Now?' In public?

'Absolutely. It's your punishment.'

It didn't feel much like a punishment.

In the crowded club, the music thumped. In no way were they the only couple doing the bump and grind. It looked like dancing. It was dancing. Except he was expertly rubbing her just the way he knew she liked to be rubbed. And in less than thirty seconds she was hurtling to the place only he could send her.

She stumbled. His grip tightened.

Heat enveloped her. Her mind a haze. She no longer cared about who could see them. What his family or anyone else would think. She was with James. He was all that mattered. And she was burning up for him. He knew it. She saw the smile and satisfaction in his eyes—the blind, glazed look of escape into physical pleasure. All that did was stoke her higher. She wanted him to be happy. She wanted to give him the relief that he brought her.

'Take me home,' she begged.

He kissed her. Bending her back so she had to cling to

him, pushing her hips right into his, thrusting his hungry tongue deep into her mouth.

His eyes glittered as he lifted his head and looked down at her. 'Yes.'

James didn't care what Jack or George or anyone thought as he walked out of the club with Caitlin clamped to his side. But Jack, true brother that he was, didn't ask, he just walked with them outside, flagged a cab and held the door open.

'George and I'll come home later.' He closed it on them.

In the cab, James turned towards Caitlin, needing her kiss more than he needed air. His thoughts went chaotic as she kissed him back. This was crazy. He *knew* this was crazy. But he needed her more than he'd ever needed any woman. He ached to find release in her arms. Since he'd told her about Louis and Pete this morning, the need had burned even more out of control.

He'd seen people thrown together in drastic circumstances, who'd believed they'd forged a relationship so strong nothing could ever break it. But things did. Ordinary life did.

This thing with Caitlin was too soon. Too built on *sex*. It was nothing more than an affair—like a schoolboy crush. His inability to think of anything other than her was symptomatic of that. A fixation that wouldn't stand the test of time. It would fade. He couldn't believe in it, couldn't start to dream of all the things he'd long ago sworn to deny himself.

But there wasn't just lust in her eyes. Not only lascivious hunger. There was tease, yes, but also tenderness. Passion, but also patience. She was generous and gentle.

He held her hand tightly as he walked through the quiet, dark house, taking her to his bedroom. She belonged in his bed.

Her skin glowed, her shoulders creamy and smooth. She

bared herself, touching him, offering herself—for him to use her as he wanted. He didn't want to use her. Didn't want to take up the dare she'd made on the dance floor. Because he wanted to touch her too, wanted to see her smile. Wanted to see her happy. More than anything.

He shuddered as she touched him. Closed his eyes against the overwhelming burst of emotion that flared within him. *Damn it.*

For an instant he tried to deny it. He didn't want the intensity that was beginning to override their time together. He just wanted sex, right? The fun, meaningless kind. He sought nothing but satisfaction. Not any kind of connection, none of this 'opening up'. They weren't sharing on that level. He'd been wrong to tell her about Louis.

He kept his eyes closed, so she was only curves and heat and softness. But there was no denying it was Caitlin. Caitlin's sighs, Caitlin arching against him. Welcoming him. Accepting him. Holding nothing back from him—offering it all. And he couldn't resist taking it.

On the beach today he'd known she wouldn't let him down—she'd listened. Accepted. And now she embraced.

Wasn't that why he'd told her? Because he'd known she would hold him anyway.

He felt as if he were tearing apart. He pressed kisses to the junction of her neck and shoulder, wrapped his arms tightly about her to hold her close. She clung back—held him—as they both trembled and tumbled over the edge.

His lungs worked hard—unable to catch the breath he so badly needed. She'd let him claim her. And in her unquestioning acceptance of his demands, she'd damn well given him so much more again. And he'd given her more than he wanted to.

There was nothing simple about what they shared.

There was nothing simple about anything any more.

CHAPTER ELEVEN

A GENTLE KNOCK at the door woke Caitlin.

'James?'

It was Jack.

James covered her with the sheet and wrapped a towel round his waist. From the bed Caitlin couldn't decipher the soft murmurs, but she saw the concerned look in Jack's eye. Saw the way he handed James something. A loyal brother.

James didn't look pleased as he came back to bed after saying bye to Jack and closing the door. He was carrying an iPad. That was what Jack had given him? Caitlin's blood iced. Over his shoulder, she stared at the screen. She blinked rapidly, but the picture didn't change.

The photo was basically explicit. You could see the outline of her nipples—diamond hard—her lips were red and swollen from James' kisses. Her cheeks were flushed as she walked pressed close to his side, her hand locked in his as they exited the club last night. He wore the edgy, almost violent expression of a man about to stake his sexual claim.

It hadn't helped that he'd pulled her onto his lap the second they'd got into the cab outside the nightclub. In that second picture there weren't hands in inappropriate places, but it was clear what was about to occur.

She looked at the logo of the British tabloid in the top corner of the webpage. Of course. Even a former E-list celebrity like her gave them fodder to fill their poisonous on-line editions. Frustration spurted in a furious blast. It wasn't as if she courted publicity. If only she'd not gotten involved with Dominic. It wasn't fair.

Through blurry eyes she read parts of the accompanying article—and the comments people had left at the bottom of it.

Beauty and the Bitch.
Someone needs to warn him...the most unlikely couple...
Scarred hero will be screwed over by the psycho.

All the venom was there. The vile things people said, carping about him being with her. Some celebrity psychologist had even done a boxed opinion piece on 'why do the good guys always want to redeem wayward women?'. The opposite of the good-girls going for bad-boys. Somehow, it was always the woman's fault. The good girls were labelled stupid for thinking they could change someone. Yet the good guy was heroic for trying to pull back the titanium-tits bitch.

'I'm sorry.' James switched the screen to black. 'Don't look at it. Don't go there.'

'I don't understand how they knew we were there.' Horrified, she stared at him.

His brows drew together and he stared back at her. 'Don't think I told them.'

'You didn't?'

He looked appalled. Then irate. 'Like I'd let the media know anything. Did you?'

'Of course not,' she spat.

'Why are we fighting?' He grasped her wrist as she tried to leave the bed. 'This is ridiculous. We both loathe the intrusion. Neither of us would sell our souls, right?'

'Right.' She drew in a shaky breath. 'Sorry. Of course you didn't tell them. It just threw me.'

She knew some other story would soon take its place. It was like being stabbed—sudden and sharp—and everyone's shocked eyes were locked on her as they watched the blood ooze. But they'd soon turn away, as soon as some other attention-worthy mess occurred. But she'd be left with the wound. It lingered with her far longer. It wasn't fifteen minutes of fame in the Internet, more like five seconds. And yet it was then up there for all eternity. Any time someone did a search, it would be found again. She'd never truly be able to escape it.

'It probably wasn't even paparazzi,' James said. 'Everyone has a smartphone these days, right?'

There was no such thing as privacy.

'I'm not even famous,' she whispered. 'Why does anyone give a damn? I'm not news.'

But she was the villain-du-jour. And James? James was the hero.

'It doesn't matter,' he said shortly. 'Forget about it.'

He spoke with such crisp authority. As if it really were that easy. Maybe for him it was.

'Oh, sure.' She painted on a smile. 'I'll do that.'

When she went down to breakfast she swore she saw caution in his parents' eyes as they greeted her. They'd read the story too. It had rehashed the worst of the Dominic nightmare. The accusations of cattiness, craziness, vindictiveness. Her brief moment of being no one, of having no past and reputation to cloud their minds and poison their perceptions, that was gone. Now they knew she wasn't the woman for their precious son. The one they so obviously wanted to care for and protect and to see happy.

James was quiet again. She felt the old isolation return.

At three a.m. they'd still been awake, clinging to each other in wild abandon, but now?

It meant nothing. Now, more than ever, she understood it had to mean nothing.

She wasn't the right woman for him. She didn't need the trolls on the Internet to tell her that.

Mid-morning he walked over to her as she sat on one of the wicker chairs on the deck, staring out to the sea. 'You're still worried.'

'Your family have read those stories.' She couldn't bring herself to even look at his mother.

'And my family knows those kinds of stories are fiction.'

Mostly. But there was the 'no smoke without fire' thing. The partial truth. 'You're not going to ask me about it?' she said softly.

He hunched down before her. 'You already told me you've never been pregnant.'

'And you truly believed me? Just like that?'

'Why? You want to me to find a lie detector? Do some torture?' He smiled and shook his head. 'If that's what you say, then I believe you.'

He'd not asked her about it directly since that day they'd Googled each other. She'd told him the truth. And he'd accepted it. She hadn't needed to pull out all kinds of exhibits or evidence to be believed. He hadn't needed it. Or wanted it. Still didn't.

She almost smiled. 'I should explain it to your parents.'

'Leave it.' He shook his head. 'You don't need to explain anything to anyone.' He lifted a hand and ran his fingers through his hair. 'No one can really understand what someone else might be going through. No one should make judgments. Your body, your life, the way you choose to live it. That's your choice. What decisions you make, or may have made, you'll have your reasons for them.'

'Some of my choices have been wrong,' she said. 'They've been mistakes.'

'Me too, you *know* that,' he whispered. 'So we just have to try to learn from them, right? Not repeat them.' He looked at her, his eyes shadowed but sure. 'And not keep beating ourselves up about them for the rest of our lives.'

Her heart melted. He might be as human as she, might have made big mistakes, but he was undeniably courageous. And so easy to want to love.

'Come on,' he said, standing up and drawing away. 'I think it's time we went back to Manhattan.'

Half an hour later his parents were still all polite smiles as they stood on the driveway to wave them off.

'I'll come back again soon.' James wrapped his mother in a hug. 'Before I go overseas for a while again. Okay?'

He felt his mother's arms tighten. 'We'd love that.'

'Me too.' He smiled and pressed a quick kiss on her hair. Actually meaning it. And actually feeling okay. The old aching lump in his heart was still there, but for some reason it had softened a smidge.

He glanced at Caitlin waiting in the passenger seat already. She looked pale, as if she hadn't slept. Well, he knew for a fact she hadn't.

He'd take her back to the condo. It had been a mistake to bring her here. A mistake to take her out last night. He kept seeing that photo from that website. The one where he was holding her close and all but dragging her out of the club. He hardly recognised himself—the expression on his face was one of total ownership.

Since when did he act so 'Me Tarzan. You Jane'? Was it when she'd asked *him* to take her *home*? Like they belonged *together*?

His muscles twitched. They'd hardly started the cruise through the villages when his mobile rang. He glanced at

the screen and immediately pulled over to take the call.
'Lisbet?'

'You know how you didn't want the full two weeks off?'

His adrenalin spiked as he heard the catch of anxiety in
Lisbet's voice. 'Yeah?'

'It's that conference.'

'You need me to go?' James asked before she could even
explain her reasons.

'Yes. It's just that—'

'It's no problem,' James assured her, his blood pumping.
Perfect. Breathing space. Business. Normality. 'I can do it.
As soon as you need me, I'm there.'

'Really?'

Yeah, he wasn't surprised that she was taken aback given
she knew how much he hated conferences and the whole
public-speaking thing.

'Of course.' He tried to joke. 'I'm assuming you've written the keynote?'

'I'll email it to you.'

'And I'll amend it.' He cracked a smile.

'Are you sure?'

'Don't worry,' he reassured her. 'I can do it.'

'You'll need to get the next flight to Sapporo.' The anxiety returned to Lisbet's voice.

'Have you booked me a ticket already?'

'I'm on it now. I'll email it. You've only got a couple
hours.'

'Great,' he said. 'JFK?' He'd have to drop Caitlin off
and go straight there.

'Yes.' Her relief was audible. 'I knew I could rely on
you. Thank you.'

'Not a problem. You do what you have to do. And so
will I.'

'I will.'

James rang off and pulled back out into the traffic lane before saying anything to Caitlin. He pressed hard on the accelerator. This was a good thing. It'd give him a few days to pause and get his head together. Caitlin would still be in New York when he got back and he'd see how things were then. He glanced at her. She was watching the scenery whizz by.

'Did you get the gist of that?' he asked.

'You're going somewhere.' She turned her face to look at him, concern etched in her blue eyes. 'Has something horrible happened somewhere?'

'No, thank goodness.' He hurriedly smiled, hating the spasm of guilt that she'd been worried for a moment. It reinforced his instinct—he was right to walk away. 'I have to go to that conference in Northern Japan.'

Her eyes widened. 'There really *is* a conference? I thought you just made that up as an excuse to fob off your family.'

'There really is a conference.' He chuckled, even as he felt another bite of that guilt. 'At the time it was also an excuse because I didn't have to go to it. Now I do.'

'Oh.'

'It's a big conference. Important. I have to deliver the keynote.'

'Wow.'

'Hmm.' He glanced at her again. She was back to looking at the scenery. 'Not my favourite thing to do,' he said. 'But I really do have to—'

'It's okay, you don't have to explain it, I understand.' Caitlin *totally* understood.

James had a job to do. And that job always came first.

She breathed in, trying to get her head around the sudden change of plan. There'd been no hesitation in his replies during the call. He'd *offered* instantly. Absolute readiness and pleasure. No thought for what—or who—he'd be leaving behind. He'd just locked into action-man mode. It was what he loved.

All he loved.

Oh, she was stupid. So lame to have been so looking forward to getting back to the condo and having him to herself again.

That she'd come to feel so much for him so quickly? The clichés were clichés for a reason—they were true. Prolonged physical intimacy led to emotional entanglement. For her anyway. Had she really thought that the almost desperate way he'd held her to him last night had meant something? What a fool she was.

She stared resolutely out of the window. Refusing to let herself feel any kind of hurt. Impossible of course. And she didn't want him to go. She didn't want him to leave her.

But he was. After all, what was a few more days with her compared to his work? A 'keynote speech' had to be delivered—oooh, so important.

She couldn't help the bitchy turn of her thoughts. He hadn't been called to a desperate life-saving search in the rubble somewhere hellish. This was a *conference*. A bunch of people standing round and talking.

But she wasn't going to tell him how she felt about it. As if she'd make such a fool of herself? She couldn't turn harpy on him for doing his job. She couldn't cry and say she'd miss him—which she wanted to do and would. Hell, this was a *holiday fling*—he'd probably laugh at her. Then run a mile from the psycho clinging woman. He'd think she was all that Dominic had claimed—the woman who refused to let a man walk when he wanted to.

She was the loser for taking this too seriously. She was the loser for letting him inside—not to her body, but her heart. But she'd never let him know what a fool she'd been.

Because even if he didn't laugh, the last thing she wanted now was any kind of pity.

'I'll drop you at the condo, then I'll head straight to the airport.' He broke the silence.

'You don't have to pack?'

'I have all I need with me.'

Of course. Combat pants and grey T-shirts. 'You always have your passport with you?'

'Yeah.' He nodded, his eyes fixed on the road ahead. 'You never know when you might get a call.'

'Of course.'

He really was action man. She froze inside as she listened to him. He was excited. Of course he was. Off to Japan. Off to meet with other heroic beings.

He'd obviously forgotten what was currently splattered all over the Internet—the conjecture, the criticism. He didn't care about that anyway. Of course he didn't. None of it would stick to him. But to her?

'Stay in the condo. Keep on sightseeing,' he said.

As if she wanted to do that *alone*? As if she wanted to sleep in that big bed by herself? 'Thanks.'

That was when she realised it.

The headlines were right. She *was* selfish. She wanted more, more, *Moore*. Always had. Probably always would. She wanted to be *first* in someone's life. For once. Just once. But that she'd imagined even for a moment that it could have been *him*?

The drive back to Manhattan flew by in half the time it had taken to get to the Hamptons only those two days ago. It was with utter relief that she saw his building come into view. She could hold it together for only a little longer.

As soon as he pulled over, she grabbed her bag and stepped out of the car. 'You'd better go,' she said husky and quick. 'You don't want to miss your flight.'

'Caitlin—'

'Go,' she interrupted. She didn't want to hear any kind of platitude. She waved and turned away. A split second later she turned back.

But just like that, he was gone.

CHAPTER TWELVE

PART OF THE condo was almost complete—the kitchen. In the couple of days they'd had away the builders had installed the cabinetry and the beautiful marble slab for the counter. Caitlin barely glanced at it as she dashed upstairs. She flung herself face down in pillow mountain and let the tears fall from her eyes.

Five minutes. Five minutes of moping. Then she was pulling herself together.

But she hurt so much inside. She squeezed her eyes shut. It didn't make the world go away. What an idiot. She sat up and scrubbed the tears from her face with her palms. She looked around the lovely room. Then her gaze rested on the slim black rectangle he'd left on the beside table.

It was the last thing she should do. She knew that. But she couldn't help it. She might as well see the worst. She switched it on and opened up the Internet.

Yeah. There it was. Caitlin swallowed and quickly closed down the programme. Put the iPad back. Then stood and raced to the bathroom. But as if she could run away from it at all? How could she hide from that?

How could it be that this latest round of Internet abuse upset her more than the mess with Dominic? Why was the public pillory worse this time?

Because this time it was true.

Caitlin wasn't good enough for James. He was too good for her. But not only that, he didn't feel the same about her. Once more she'd put her hopes in someone who cared more for his career than he did for her. Would she never learn?

Now she was left to deal with it alone. Again.

She couldn't stay here. She refused to take what he'd offered her. It wasn't enough. The question was where she was going to go.

She'd never ask her father for money. Or Hannah. She'd never be a leech. Hannah mightn't see it like that, but so many others definitely would. And Caitlin wasn't giving anyone any reason to doubt her—especially the sister that she'd seen so little of. With Caitlin working so much as a kid, and Hannah so much since, they'd really never had a normal kind of sibling relationship. Not the teasing and laughing James had with his brothers. She wished she could be a better sister, but for Hannah's sake Caitlin believed it was better to be an absent sister. Then she could pretend it didn't hurt so much.

She stared at her reflection and told herself to suck it up. She'd known she couldn't call on the little family she had, and she'd known she shouldn't fall for James. It just wasn't going to happen for her.

She was going to have to figure her own way through her finances, through her heartbreak. To do that she needed to go back to London as soon as she could. She'd find a job. She'd survive. She was smart. She could sew. She was strong.

She could come up with a plan.

Four days later James landed back at JFK airport. Shattered again after another flight with no sleep. But that didn't matter. He had to get home asap. He had a bad feeling. He'd called the landline at the condo several times while he was away—at the oddest of times.

She'd never picked up.

He paid off the cabbie and raced inside. The refurbished kitchen in the condo looked beautiful. But empty. The whole place felt empty.

'Caitlin?' He ran up the stairs, his heart thudding.

He didn't want this. But he already knew. His sanctuary of a bedroom was empty. And huge. And lonely. His massive bed was made—the covers unrumpled. As if they'd never been touched.

Cold.

He didn't need to look in the wardrobe to check for her clothes. She was gone. Then he saw it—the note she'd left on top of his pile of damn T-shirts.

Thanks so much, I had a fabulous holiday.

James swore. What the hell was that? Some courteous note a schoolgirl might write? It was so *nothing*.

His chest burned as if he'd been overdoing a sprints session. He'd underestimated how much he'd been looking forward to seeing her again. Now panic seized him as it hit him. He'd been *aching* to see her. Only he hadn't realised it. Hadn't let himself. But now? Now he knew he'd been missing her every waking and sleeping moment. And he wanted to see her. He wanted her here—right now, giving him one of her defiant, teasing looks as she cut him down to size with one of her quips. And he wanted her flushed and sparkling and welcoming him with her warm body—all the while still teasing him in the way only she did.

He wanted that warmth. That acerbic wit. All the spirit and generosity that was in that woman. Only Caitlin.

Now it really hit. Just how far he'd fallen. How much he wanted her. Needed her. Loved her.

And she wasn't here.

Where had she gone? Was she okay? He didn't even have her phone number. So how the hell was he going to find her now?

He grabbed his phone and called George. 'I need Hannah Moore's number.'

'Really?'

'Urgently.'

'Okay.' George caught the desperation. 'I'll get it to you.'

Less than three minutes later James' phone chimed with a text. A number. He didn't care what time it was wherever in the world Hannah was right now, James was calling.

A woman answered after five interminable rings. 'Hello?'

'Hey, is this Hannah Moore?'

'Who is this?' she asked, all frigid caution.

'Don't hang up.' James clenched his empty fist in frustration. 'I really need to find Caitlin.'

'Caitlin?'

'Your sister.' He spoke through gritted teeth.

'Who *is* this?'

'Look, my name's James Wolfe. I'm George Wolfe's twin. I met Caitlin when she came to New York and I—'

'She's in New York?'

James paused. Stunned. 'You didn't know that?'

'No, I—'

'When did you last talk to Caitlin?' Fury rose in him. And it was obvious Hannah heard it.

'Look, I'm really sorry,' she said in a far too quiet voice. 'I don't know where she is.'

'Well, would your father know?'

There was a pause. 'He's with me. And no. He doesn't know.' Another pause. 'I really am sorry.'

'You should be,' James snapped. 'All this crap she's been through and you don't even know where she is?'

'She doesn't tend to get in touch much.'

'Do you try to? Or is it just easier for you to leave her out in the cold?'

Irate, James ended the call. He was appalled at the fact that her own damn family had no idea where she was. Was it that they really didn't care? Or were they too bound up in their own business? Either way it wasn't good enough.

His heart burned. She deserved so much more than that. She deserved to be loved. Damn it. He'd love her.

Just as soon as he could find her.

He glanced round the bedroom once more. His iPad was on the bedside table. He snatched it up. The Internet browser opened on the last site it had been on. James froze as he read the headline. He clicked back a few pages in the history file.

Shit.

That stupid picture of him and Caitlin. Those wretched people with nothing better to do. It had bothered him—because of what he'd seen on his own face. But it had bothered Caitlin for a whole other reason.

Oh, God, he was such an idiot.

Once again she'd had been left to deal with something like this alone—the vitriol, the painful words. No wonder she'd run. All her life she'd lacked emotional support. And James had failed her too.

He was useless.

He breathed in and tried to think. *Where* would she go? In a city of millions, where would he find her?

CHAPTER THIRTEEN

CAITLIN WALKED THROUGH the studio, amazed all over again at the incredible sight of so many people—tailors, seamstresses, milliners and assistants working to get the hundreds of costumes required ready.

She'd done the necessary. Rebooked her return flight—sucking up the change fee—so she'd be back in London by the end of the week. Then she'd crossed her fingers that Peggy didn't read the trash on Twitter. She contacted her and asked if she could take her up on that offer to see the costume department.

So here she was. At the Met costume studio, blown away by the skill and expertise, the vast vaults of costumes stored so they could restage a previous production. It was like Aladdin's cave, or the lost tomb of Cleopatra or something—filled with treasures and inspiration. She spent a couple of hours being shown around by an assistant as jazzed about the place as she was.

It was exactly what she'd needed.

But once her visit ended, she went to the station and boarded a train to Queens. She'd found the cheapest hostel she could, sharing a dorm with five strangers. She'd barely slept these last few nights. Not because of the noise of the trains on the tracks right next door, but because the minute she closed her eyes, she thought of James.

The sooner she got back to London, the better. Whatever it took, she'd get herself back together. Seeing that costume studio today had spurred her. She'd build a career. And she'd get on with it. Alone. Independent.

She walked up the stairs into the hostel, going straight up to the first floor. She passed the other dorm-room doors—hers was the last.

'Caitlin?'

She froze partway down the corridor, then turned.

'James?' She stared at him in total confusion. But she wasn't imagining things. He really was there—all stubble and smoky eyes and crumpled grey tee. 'What are you doing here?'

Why was he here and looking so fabulous and intense and magnetic just when she was kidding herself she could get over him?

'What do you think?' he exploded, taking five energy-filled strides closer. 'Finding you.'

Oh. She swallowed.

'You left,' he accused.

No. *He'd* left. 'I left a note,' she said coldly.

'That told me nothing.'

'What do you want to know?'

'That you're okay. For starters.'

Of course he did. Mr Hero himself. 'Well, as you can see, I'm okay.' She struggled to pull herself together. 'I'm sorry, I didn't mean to worry you. I didn't think that—' *He'd care.*

His lips compressed. 'You have a shockingly low opinion of me. And an even worse one of yourself.' He glanced behind her and frowned.

Caitlin turned and saw another traveller walking towards them. James wrapped a hand around her upper arm. She flinched and turned back to face him. His fingers instantly loosened, stroked, but then he walked, urging her to come into the room with him.

She did, knowing it was better to have this conversation with some degree of privacy. It wasn't a dorm room, but a tiny space with room for only a bed and a chair. Single occupancy. Double at a squeeze. Nothing like the magnificent room they'd shared in his condo.

'Of course I was worried about you.' He shut the door and turned to her. His face was paler than usual, it made the line of his scar all the more obvious. 'You're not interested in whether I'm okay?'

'I can see that you are.' She tried to shrug.

'Do I *really* look okay to you?'

She glanced back at him swiftly. He sounded angry. Well, she was fast joining him on that one. She didn't want him here. Didn't want him feeling as if he had to ensure she was 'okay'. That wasn't anywhere near enough for her. And she sure as hell didn't want him thinking he could pick up where they'd left off. No way could she touch him again—the fling was flung. And just because they were in a bedroom again, didn't mean she was going to let him—

'What's the problem?' She yanked on the toughest shell she could. 'Blue balls?'

'Caitlin.'

To her annoyance, the man smiled.

No. She wasn't letting him do this to her. She wasn't falling for his charm again. For his tease and flirt. For his gorgeousness and good humour and generosity.

It wasn't enough.

There was only one thing she could do—push him away. Hard. Fast. For ever.

'Look, it was just sex, James,' she said as blithely as she could. 'That convenient holiday-fling thing. We were sharing the room, why not have a few frolics at the same time?'

He stared at her. To her discomfort, his expression only grew even more amused.

'Oh, Caitlin.'

'Don't go thinking it was anything special.' She shook her head and backed up as he walked towards her. The backs of her legs bumped against the metal-framed bed.

'You think you can do the bad-girl act and push me away?'

'It's no act. I am what I am.' She shrugged, curling her damp fingers into fists.

'Nothing is black and white. No one is a stereotype. You're not all bad girl. And I'm sure as hell not all hero.'

But he was. He so was. He couldn't help himself.

'You know I'm far from perfect,' he reminded her.

She switched tack. 'Quite right. I was getting bored already.'

'That so?'

'Yeah. I'm ready to change it up.'

He took the last pace to stand directly in front of her. Reached for her. 'You think some other guy can turn you on the way I do?'

She stood like a stone, refusing to move. To *be* moved. 'So we do good sex,' she said crassly. 'We can make each other come in record speed. So what? You can't construct a relationship built on something so ephemeral. So meaningless.'

His eyes gleamed. He didn't seem bothered by her crude bluntness. 'It's a starting point.' He was too calm. Being too damn reasonable.

She didn't want him to be reasonable. She wanted to push him away. Had to push him. 'But it's sand, not rock. Sexual appetite will wash away. And there's nothing else to us. There never has been.'

He put his head on the side, ran his hands down her arms. 'You really want me to believe that?'

Caitlin's heart stopped. To believe her? To believe in her *lies*? She suppressed all the pain. But she'd suppressed too much pain, for too long. 'It doesn't matter to me what you believe,' she choked.

'So you're going to walk away?'

'I'm not walking away from anything much.' Blinking, she determinedly stuck to her line, wishing like crazy that *he'd* walk away right now. 'A bit of sex. A few laughs. But that's it. There's nothing more to this and never has been.'

'People might have accused you of all kinds of things, but I never thought you were a coward,' he said quietly.

'I'm *not* a coward.' She shook with defiance. She wasn't. She'd tried and tried and she'd keep on trying.

'Yes, you are,' he said softly. 'You run. You hide. You won't stand up and say what's really true. What you really *feel*. What you really *want*.' His hands slipped up and gripped her shoulders. 'And I don't blame you for that. You've been hurt. Your dad. Hannah. Dominic. And me.'

Caitlin bit on the inside of her lip. Hard. Stupid when she was already trying to blink back tears. But she had to stop herself from speaking. From breaking down.

'I hurt you.' He stepped forward, right into her space so she could feel his heat. His rock-solid strength. 'I left you when you needed me. And I'm sorry. It won't happen again.'

She stared up at him—at his dark, dark, beautiful eyes. She tried to swallow the lump of jagged glass in her throat.

'Caitlin.'

She closed her eyes. 'Please leave.'

'No.'

'Please leave. Now.'

'No.'

Couldn't he do that for her? Couldn't he leave her with

that illusion of dignity before she sank to the floor and howled? She opened her burning eyes and pleaded.

'I can't do this,' she begged him. 'Please don't ask me to do this.'

'Don't try to push me away. It won't work.'

'I'm trying to do the right thing,' she whispered.

'Then do the right thing, the right way.'

And what was the right thing?

She knew already. Being honest. Being brave. Speaking up.

'What is it you really want?' he asked softly. 'Tell me what you really want.'

She licked away a tear that had tumbled down to her lips. A pointless action as several more immediately followed the track of the first.

'Caitlin?'

She knew that look on his face. He wanted to kiss her. He wanted to hold her close. More than anything she wanted that too. But she couldn't. She was too selfish. And he needed to know that.

'I want *you*,' she cried. 'But I can't have you. Not the way I want. I can't cope with being left alone time and time again. I know it's pathetic of me. I know what you do is so important. Much more important than anything else. Than me.' She dragged in a jerky breath. 'But I don't want to stop you doing what you have to. What kind of person would I be if I tried? I can't—'

'Stop.' He slid his hands from her shoulders down her back to her waist, pulling her close, cradling her against him. 'It's okay. Darling, it's going to be okay.'

'It's not. It can't be.' Her words were muffled against his chest. She wanted him here for her—all for her. And he couldn't be.

'I would do anything for you,' he breathed into her ear.

'Listen to me. Anything.' He bent his forehead to hers. 'If you asked me to walk away from my job, I'd do it in a heartbeat.'

Her hand fisted in his shirt. 'I'd never ask you to do that.'

'I know.'

'I'm sorry,' she said, lifting her head, trying to get a grip on herself. 'I want too much. It's not right how much I want from you.'

'Sure it is. It's okay to want it all from me.' His smile was crooked and sweet and heartbreaking. 'Don't just demand what you want from me in bed, but in everything. Ask me for it all. Because all I have to give is yours.'

She shook her head.

He moved, quickly framing her face with gentle hands— stopping her from denying him.

'I've never felt so empty as when I got home and you weren't there,' he said, a hurried low tumble of words. 'I haven't felt that afraid in a long, long time.'

Caitlin swallowed hard.

'I thought I had it all figured,' he said. 'That I was okay. That I'd worked everything through in my past, found the career I could live for. That I was happy. But you were right in that I'd gone too far in that direction. I'd isolated myself—shut out my family. I had no idea I was lonely. I was using work—all that travel—to plug a hole I didn't realise was there. Then *you* landed, claiming that spot, filling the emptiness, warming me. I want you back there.'

'Not *me*.' She shook her head. 'It's just you needed a holiday—'

'No.' His sharp laugh broke in the middle. 'I needed *you*. Your challenge, your determination, your humour. Your laughter. You woke me up. Warmed me up. Made me realise everything I've been missing. And everything that I want. It's all you.'

'But—'

He kissed her. Deeply, sweetly. Lovingly.

Caitlin had no chance. She sank into it, already lost. He'd come for her—for all of her.

'I'm not going to leave you again,' he said.

He'd given her everything. Only now she knew she couldn't accept it. 'You *have* to. You have places to go. People to help.'

'There are plenty of people to help in New York.'

She shook her head. 'You love what you do.'

'Okay.' He nodded. 'I do. But I can find a different balance. Because I love you more.'

Caitlin trembled, the tears instantly springing to her eyes again. It was the one thing she'd never thought she'd hear from anyone. And to hear it from him?

'Stay in New York.' He urged her closer with hands and words and heat. 'Find a job in a theatre. Design costumes. Stay with me.'

Warmth exploded in her chest. He meant it—he wanted her, needed her, loved her. Her courageous, generous man. And suddenly she felt strengthened. *Secure.*

Suddenly she knew she could share him, because she understood he'd always come home to her.

'I love you.' She put her hand to his face. 'And I will stay. I'll love you. And I'll be there for you when you get back. But you have to keep doing your assignments.'

He gazed at her, his cocoa eyes searching, softening. 'Not as many,' he said. 'There are other things I need too— time with my family. Time with you. And that's okay.'

'Yes.'

'But what if…?' He paused and drew in a juddering breath. 'What if you sometimes came with me? I know it's not easy, but you could help in so many ways,' he said in a rush. 'Make clothes? Entertain people? Give a couple of kids something to smile at? Just offer comfort? Chocolate? Hell.' He drew another breath. 'Be there for me.'

She'd go anywhere for him. 'I'd like that.'

He kissed her again. His hands pressed her closer, his hold tightening almost enough to crush her. She loved it.

'We'll stay outside the spotlight,' he continued, that loveable wicked look lighting his eyes. 'No scandal. Just a boring loved-up couple.'

He was offering it all to her. No longer alone, she had the one person she needed most. The one person who believed in her. Who saw worth in her. Who wanted to be with her more than he wanted anything else.

She lifted her hand to his face. 'You couldn't be boring if you tried.'

He chuckled, his hands sliding over her curves again— less of a cuddle now. Way more carnal. 'Nor can you.'

She wriggled closer. 'We'll create our own, personal outrageous headlines, right?'

'What are you thinking?' His voice dropped into wicked territory.

'I'm thinking, *Couple Break Hostel Bed.*'

James threw his head back and laughed. 'Because of vigorous and energetic sex?' He put his hands on her hips and tugged her tight against him. 'What about *Former Teen Soap Star's Three Day Love-In at City Hostel.* And of course, *Hostel Occupants Complain About Loud Screams of Ecstasy.*'

Giggling, Caitlin nodded enthusiastically.

'So what do you say?' He waggled his eyebrows.

Caitlin knew there was only one answer and it had to be shouted multiple times.

'Yes! Yes! Yes!'

* * * * *

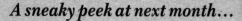

A sneaky peek at next month...

MODERN
tempted™

**FRESH, CONTEMPORARY ROMANCES TO TEMPT
ALL LOVERS OF GREAT STORIES**

My wish list for next month's titles...

In stores from 18th October 2013:

❏ What the Bride Didn't Know — Kelly Hunter

❏ Mistletoe Not Required — Anne Oliver

In stores from 1st November 2013:

❏ His Until Midnight — Nikki Logan

❏ The One She Was Warned About — Shoma Narayanan

Available at WHSmith, Tesco, Asda, Eason, Amazon and Apple

Just can't wait?

1013/3

Come home this Christmas to Fiona Harper

From the author of *Kiss Me Under the Mistletoe* comes a Christmas tale of family and fun. Two sisters are ready to swap their Christmases—the busy super-mum, Juliet, getting the chance to escape it all on an exotic Christmas getaway, whilst her glamorous work-obsessed sister, Gemma, is plunged headfirst into the family Christmas she always thought she'd hate.

www.millsandboon.co.uk

Wrap up warm this winter with Sarah Morgan...

Sleigh Bells in the Snow

Kayla Green loves business and hates Christmas.

So when Jackson O'Neil invites her to Snow Crystal Resort to discuss their business proposal... the last thing she's expecting is to stay for Christmas dinner. As the snowflakes continue to fall, will the woman who doesn't believe in the magic of Christmas finally fall under its spell...?

4th October

www.millsandboon.co.uk/sarahmorgan